THE
SNOWS

THE SNOWS

SHARELLE BYARS MORANVILLE

HENRY HOLT AND COMPANY ∼ *New York*

I'm grateful for family stories and personal recollections that inspired certain parts of *The Snows*. Special thanks to my husband, Barry, and my sister, Cathy. And I'm *always* grateful for the talent and support of my editor, Christy.

Henry Holt and Company, LLC
Publishers since 1866
175 Fifth Avenue
New York, New York 10010
www.HenryHoltKids.com

Library of Congress Cataloging-in-Publication Data
Moranville, Sharelle Byars.
The snows / Sharelle Byars Moranville.—1st ed.
p.   cm.
Summary: With the thread of family that connects them through the
generations, Jim, Cathy, Jill, and Mona each find "sixteen" to be the
pivotal age in their lives.
ISBN-13: 978-0-8050-7469-7 / ISBN-10: 0-8050-7469-4
[1. Coming of age—Fiction.   2. Interpersonal relations—Fiction.   3. Iowa—
History—20th century—Fiction.]   I. Title.
PZ7.M78825Sn 2007   [Fic]—dc22   2006035468

First edition—2007 / Designed by Laurent Linn
Printed in the United States of America on acid-free paper. ∞
10   9   8   7   6   5   4   3   2   1

To my husband, Barry

THE
SNOWS

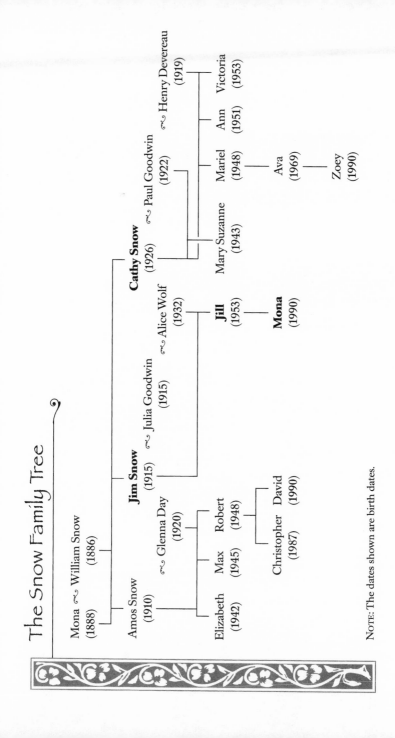

The Snow Family Tree

Mona ∾ William Snow
(1888)   (1886)

Jim Snow   **Cathy Snow**
(1915)   (1926)
∾ Julia Goodwin   ∾ Paul Goodwin
  (1915)   (1922)
∾ Alice Wolf   ∾ Henry Devereau
  (1932)   (1919)

Amos Snow
(1910)
∾ Glenna Day
  (1920)

Elizabeth   Max   Robert
(1942)   (1945) (1948)

Christopher   David
(1987)   (1990)

Jill
(1953)

Mona
(1990)

Mary Suzanne   Mariel   Ann   Victoria
(1943)   (1948)   (1951) (1953)

Ava
(1969)

Zoey
(1990)

NOTE: The dates shown are birth dates.

Contents

Jim
1931

Chapter One

CATHY CAME RUNNING across the yard. "Jim!" she called to me.

My little sister smelled faintly of flowers and had bits of lilac tangled in her thin, whitish yellow hair. Her skirt was ripped at the waist, and a patch of her underpants showed through the tear.

"My dolly's a worrywart," she said, hugging me. "She said you weren't coming. You want to play with us?"

"Oh, Cathy, I'm hot and tired." But I saw the look on her face. "*However . . .*"

Cathy ran toward the lilacs that grew behind the Harkers' garage, motioning me to follow.

Mrs. Harker, in her back yard pulling diapers off the clothesline, called a greeting and waved.

"In here," Cathy said, leading the way.

3

The branches of the gnarly old lilac bushes made a natural arch against the side of the Harkers' garage. I had to stoop and walk with my knees bent, my shirt brushing against the blossoms. A towel spread in the dirt made a picnic blanket for small tin dishes, and a doll with the stuffing coming out leaned against the foundation.

"This is mine and Dolly's new house," Cathy announced. "Want to live with us?"

"Sure," I said, squatting down.

As I cradled a tiny cup of make-believe cocoa, I heard a faint voice calling, "Hel-lo-o!"

Julia.

What was she doing at our house? Our warped screen door rattled as she knocked.

"Gotta go!" I told Cathy, backing out of the narrow space.

"But you didn't eat your cookies."

I made smacking noises as I wiggled free of the lilac branches. "Thank you." Then I saw the bereft look on her face. "Race you to the porch," I offered.

Her expression cleared a little, and she grabbed her dolly by one arm and ran ahead of me. Cathy got to the porch first, just as Mama opened the screen door and stepped out, her finger tucked in her book to mark her place.

"Hello, kids." She had a red patch on her cheekbone from propping her face against her hand as she read.

The color in Julia's own face was as soft as cream. "Hello, Mrs. Snow," Julia said.

I still couldn't believe I'd kissed Julia Goodwin after the play last week. She hadn't been my date. I'd never dated a girl as grand as her. We'd simply gone out the back door of the gymnasium at the same time. I was taking a shortcut home. I'm not sure where Julia was going. The moon had been out, and the humid April air promised all kinds of things. Julia's hair had caught the moonlight, and she was only about four inches away and nobody was around and it had just happened. And after, I'd whispered, "Good night," and walked on home wondering exactly when the sky would open and the fates would strike me dead.

This afternoon, her hair shone like polished copper in the sunshine.

"I wasn't expecting you," I blurted. She'd stopped by to break off our first date for tonight. I knew it.

She handed me my English lit book. "You left this in study hall."

What if she'd seen the little torn piece of paper that marked the page where her very own name—*Julia*—was used by the seventeenth-century poet Robert Herrick in a love poem—actually, several love poems—and that I'd been reading those poems and replaying that kiss a million times in my mind?

Mama sat down in the glider and opened her book. Cathy leaned against her knees. "I'm hungry, Mama." Mama made an absentminded humming sound, but that was all. Something had scratched Cathy, and a line of blood ran down the back of her dirty arm.

Julia's eyes moved from Cathy to Mama to me. "I forgot what time you were coming over," she said.

"About seven. If that's okay."

She nodded. "See you then."

I watched her walk away, the shiny material on her skirt catching the light. I had about turned to stone by the time she stopped at the end of the block and turned, waving to me.

I waved back, and then I went to the porch, picking up Cathy and carrying her on my hip. "Did you know that peanut butter can give you magical powers?" I asked.

A few minutes later Cathy followed me up to my room with her peanut butter sandwich. She lay on the floor with her doll and colored while I sat at my old Underwood and pecked out the article Miss Paxton had asked me to write for the last issue of *The Quill*. Normally the assignment would have gone to one of the senior staff members, but in May they didn't have time, so I got the job.

A breeze from the open window touched my arm. I shut my eyes and tapped out a sentence. Thought. Listened to the silence until a Model T rattled past. Typed a little more, feeling the open-ended bliss of nothing to do for an hour or so except shape words into sentences into paragraphs. The speed of my typing picked up, erratic and enthusiastic, as if the words were applauding themselves as they came.

Cathy colored quietly, the only sound the rubbing of her crayons against the paper. Birds in the yard fussed over something.

Mulling over a sentence, I stared at the calendar. It was hanging open to May and showed a picture of a farmer planting corn, courtesy of Lindquist's Funeral Home.

Cathy came to show me her work. "Look!"

The two figures had rectangular bodies, stick limbs, and circle heads. Both wore bright red hearts on their chests.

"You and me," Cathy explained.

"I like the colors." I tried not to mind the grime that lined her fingernails. Mama's forte was great books, rather than the daily details of motherhood.

Cathy's eyes shone as if I'd given her a hundred dollars with those four words of attention. "Want to play I Spy?" she asked. "You can go first."

"I have to write. It's for school."

"Oh."

But I didn't have to write this very minute. Not for a few days, even. But I *wanted* to write this very minute. And why shouldn't I? It wasn't the most selfish thing in the world. I wasn't taking oxygen that somebody else needed.

I had the sentence almost perfect in my head when Cathy started bouncing her feet against the floor. I looked out of the corner of my eye. How could such small bare feet make so much of a racket?

Ah, she'd quit.

Back to the sentence.

"Jim?"

"What!"

Her eyes met mine with such acceptance that I knew she heard that same tone a hundred times a day from Mama, who didn't want to be bothered any more than I did.

"Cathy—"

Downstairs, the warped screen door squeaked open, then bumped closed unevenly. "Dad's home," I said, hoping she would go see him and leave me alone.

But Mama's and Dad's voices were loud enough after about three sentences for Cathy to put her hands over her ears. ". . . too much to expect a decent supper and . . ." Dad hacked his cigarette cough, and Mama's book clapped shut like thunder following a lightning bolt.

Cathy looked at me.

Shortly after, a metal pan came down hard on the top of the counter, the lid rattling. A cupboard door slammed.

Dad's voice rose. "What is this trash, Mona?"

They were more or less right below us now, in the back of the house.

"*Leaves of Grass*," Mama said. "It's *poetry*."

"It's a dirty book!"

"It's *literature*, William!"

"It's *a dirty book*! And I won't have it in the house. . . ."

Why couldn't I have half an hour of peace to write? Or even ten minutes? Or even *two* minutes? I snatched Cathy to her feet and carried her to the bathroom, trying to get away from their argument.

"Let me see that scratch on your arm," I said through clenched teeth.

The scratch looked red and irritated.

Trying to settle the fury pulsing in my veins, I made myself wait while the water running over my fingers turned slowly tepid and then warm. Cathy sat patiently on the toilet lid and stared at her feet.

The bathroom was right above the kitchen. A register in the bathroom floor allowed heat from the gravity furnace to rise in the winter. Now it let in the hot, angry smell of searing meat Mama had flung into the pan.

My hands shook as I held the warm washcloth against the cut on Cathy's arm. Dirt and blood came away, leaving a patch of pale, soft skin. She smelled like saltwater taffy.

I blew on the scratch and dabbed it with a towel, then I began to wash her face and ears and neck, feeling calmer. She gave me her grimy-nailed hands and I massaged them in the suds of the washcloth, feeling her small bones moving against one another.

As I bent down to wash Cathy's legs and feet, I felt her breath on the side of my face. I patted her feet dry, the anger flowing out of me.

"I spy something," I said. "It's a pair. The color is blue."

"Your eyes!" she said, delighted.

Actually, it was her eyes, but I didn't say anything.

By the time we got to the supper table, Dad had simmered down. He dipped boiled potatoes onto his plate. "So what's Amos got to say for himself?" He eyed the letter from my brother that Mama had leaned against the sugar bowl.

"He says he's doing some new kind of research on seed corn. He probably won't be home at all this summer. He's got a job with one of the professors." Mama laughed. "You know how Amos is. Once he gets caught up in something, the rest of the world can go hang."

Mama would know about that if anybody would.

"Want me to cut up your pork chop?" she asked Cathy, who had speared the whole piece of meat on the end of her fork and was gnawing at the edges.

Cathy's eyes lifted to Mama's.

"You look so nice and clean!" Mama marveled, noticing Cathy's scrubbed pinkness.

I sighed. If Mama would put down her books, stay home from Ladies' Reading Circle meetings, and not get so caught up in the stories and articles she enjoyed writing, she might notice Cathy's half-ripped skirt.

"Amos is fortunate," Dad said. He hacked a wet cough and went to the back door to spit.

I tried not to listen.

Dad dragged his feet onto the porch every night with the look of a man who truly hated how he'd spent his day.

Before I could stop myself, I asked, "Dad, how come you became a barber if you hate it so much?"

A look flicked between Mama and Dad as he returned to his seat and sawed away at his pork chop, his knife scraping on the plate. Mama laughed. "Somebody paid his way to barber college."

The shadows under Dad's eyes looked purple in the overhead light. He frowned. "I didn't ask your family to do that."

"Well, you didn't tell them *no* either."

Dad shrugged, giving Mama a baleful look.

"Your dad had to do something," Mama explained to me. "And my family was just thinking of our future. At least it's respectable," she reminded Dad. "You have your own shop."

"How'd you like to cut the filthy hair of farmers, son?" Dad demanded, turning to me. "Day after day?" He didn't wait for my answer. "On Saturday night they come in, their breath stinking from the onions they've eaten down at Harley's. And although the sign on the door clearly says we close at ten, they just keep coming, sometimes past midnight."

Dad always walked as if his feet hurt. They probably did. That was one reason I was going to be a writer.

I admitted, "I'd hate it."

Dad looked at Mama as if to say, See? "That's why Amos is lucky," he concluded.

"Well, what do you *want* to do, William?" Mama asked with exaggerated patience. Mama loved Dad. I could tell by the look in her eyes. But how had two such different people ever gotten together?

Dad chewed thoughtfully. Swallowed. "A grocery store would be nice."

"Why on earth a grocery store?" Mama inquired.

Dad bit off each word. "Because it's not a barbershop, Mona."

"But, Dad, the town already has grocery stores. There's—"
Dad interrupted me. "It wouldn't have to be here."

Mama's brows drew together.

"Colorado," Dad said, pulling a place out of the air, smiling. "We could open a grocery store in Colorado."

Mama was shaking her head.

If we moved to Colorado, Julia would get snatched up before I was to the Nebraska line. We *couldn't* move to Colorado. What about my summer job? My best friend, Noah, and I had jobs working at an ice cream shop.

Cathy was looking at me.

I let out my breath. What was I getting so worked up about? Dad was just talking. He was always talking. I winked at Cathy.

Mama laughed as if Dad had told a really good joke, and even Dad finally shrugged it off with a grin. He pushed his chair back from the table and lit a cigarette.

Dad's problem was that he didn't have a star to follow. Mama did. She wanted to read and discuss great ideas. Write about them. Amos had a star. He wanted to mess around with seed corn research. I had a star, too. I wanted to write. But Dad just didn't want to be a barber anymore. He was like that. He got tired of stuff.

"You want me to come down and sweep out the place for you now and then?" I asked. School would be out before long. I'd have my thirty hours or so a week of mixing and hand packing ice cream at the Cottage, but that would still leave some time. Unless Julia ended up claiming it—which was about as likely as Greta Garbo stopping in for a carry-out pint of lemon custard.

Dad blew smoke and rolled the glowing tip of the cigarette along the indentation on the ashtray. He looked at me. "Nah. That's okay, son."

Cathy slid out of her chair and held up the doll she'd been cuddling on her lap. "Will you fix her, Jim? Her stuffing's coming out."

I tried to make a joke, poking her through the rip in her dress. "Your stuffing's coming out, too."

"So will you fix her?"

"I can't right now. I gotta go someplace." The fat from the pork chop had congealed around the edge of my plate, and Dad's cigarette smoke hung in the room. I wanted to wash and brush my teeth and walk in the fresh evening air. "Maybe tomorrow," I told Cathy. Tonight, I wanted to see Julia.

A boy about nine was dribbling a basketball along the sidewalk in front of their house. I was pretty sure he was Julia's little brother. "Paul!" a woman's voice called. He gave the ball one last bounce, glanced over his shoulder at me, and ran up the steps and inside.

Julia's dad was sitting on the front porch. The sunset barely gave enough light to read, but he rocked in the porch swing, his head bent close to a folded newspaper. He looked up, surprised to see me.

"Jim Snow," he said. Mr. Goodwin never forgot anybody's name. But he looked at me with a question on his face. Was I selling pencil sharpeners for Glee Club or something?

"Hi," I said. "Is Julia here?"

"Ah. I expect she is." He stepped to the screen door and called her name.

"Coming," I heard her answer from upstairs.

"Take a seat." Mr. Goodwin pointed to a metal chair with a back that was supposed to make you think of seashells. "How's your folks?"

"Fine, thanks."

Mr. Goodwin nodded. He had that easy affability that made you feel he'd just been thinking about you a minute before and was delighted you'd turned up on his doorstep. No wonder he had a big office on the town square where he dealt in insurance and real estate.

Julia had the same ability to make you feel important and pleased with yourself. Where *was* she?

"Don't see much of Amos anymore. I guess he likes being a college boy," Mr. Goodwin mused. "Probably doing pretty good at it, too. Knowing Amos, he'll come out of college and make a bundle, despite the times."

I felt grateful to Amos for having made a good impression on Julia's dad.

What was taking her so long?

Mr. Goodwin smiled. "You could do worse than follow in Amos's footsteps."

They said Mr. Goodwin had made his own bundle in the New York stock market and had the good sense to get out in the summer of twenty-nine.

Footsteps tapped down the stairs and toward the door.

If Robert Herrick had been on that front porch when Julia came out, he would have said something about how she shamed the sun into retreat. And the sun really did seem to gasp out just one more breath, throwing a pink light across the porch, as she stood in the doorway.

I rose. I never knew night air could be so soft.

"Good to see you, Jim." Mr. Goodwin shook my hand before he vanished inside.

Julia leaned against the white balustrade that ran around the porch. "Hi," she said.

"Hello." I half sat on the railing beside her.

I wasn't a football player or senior or some great-looking guy that the girls were dying to date. And it had occurred to me that all this could be part of a competition of some kind. I'd heard she and another girl, Flo Brown, kept a tally of how many guys asked them out.

"What would you like to do?" I asked. All I'd worked up the nerve to do was ask her if I could come over tonight.

"What did you have in mind?"

I hadn't gotten very far in my planning. "We could walk over to the Odd Fellows Hall." For fifty cents a couple, we could dance to a band and drink all the punch we could hold.

As she shifted her position on the porch banister, her clothing whispered. She gazed at the toes of her shoes.

I was pretty sure Julia was a nice girl, and if her date with me was no more than a tally, she'd let me save my fifty cents and suggest we just walk around town.

In the glow from the window, I could see a look of embarrassment pass across her face. She was going to stroll around the block just enough times to count me officially.

Julia made a little motion with her feet, moving them across the porch floor. Her shoes were gray, with pointed toes and a little strap.

"I don't think these shoes would stand walking all that way out to the Odd Fellows Hall and then dancing, too," she said, her voice low with regret.

Even if I'd asked Dad to borrow the car, it wouldn't have made any difference. Julia would only have found another excuse to keep me from wasting my money. I let out my breath, feeling a chill in the night air. But I had had one kiss. And I could warm myself at that fire for a long time.

She slipped off the balustrade. "Let me go get another pair of shoes."

While she was gone, I waited, counting the spindles in the porch railing, uncertain about what a second pair of shoes boded.

When Julia got back, she wore plain brown oxfords. She carried the gray ones.

"Ready," she said.

I let out my breath and stood up. "Would you like me to carry your shoes?"

Julia smiled and handed them to me. I looped my fingers through the straps and swung my arms as we walked down the sidewalk. A shooting star cut through the sky. What a wonderful universe. Maybe no one else had carried her shoes before.

People brought their whole families to the Odd Fellows Hall on Friday night, and a little girl about Cathy's age was being danced around by her grandfather as the band played a new tune called "As Time Goes By."

Julia sat in one of the chairs placed around the edge of the room and changed her shoes. Then she stood up and I took her hand. We began to move among the dancers, my hand on her back trying to signal the steps. I felt the soft tightening movements of her muscles.

"Sorry," she murmured, as our knees bumped. "You're a really good dancer."

"You're fine," I murmured. "Just fine. Did you know there used to be a swimming pool out there?" I asked to distract myself. Everybody knew the story of how the house had been built by a local shampoo magnate at the turn of the century. He'd moved east soon after and turned the sprawling mansion over to the Methodists.

"I've seen pictures," she said. "A swimming pool and croquet court off the verandah."

She did a lot with that last word—*verandah*—tipping her head back and smiling, showing the tiny gap between her two front teeth. But her eyes were vague as she concentrated on following my lead.

The Methodists had turned the house and grounds into a shelter for wayward girls. But in our town, at least, I guess Prohibition had made girls less wayward, because—for as long as I could remember—the place had been claimed by the Odd Fellows.

Julia tripped a little and apologized with a smiling grimace that showcased that little gap. What would it be like to trace that tiny crevice with the tip of my tongue? At the thought, I actually saw sparks.

Gambling everything, I pulled her close. "Following the steps will be easier," I murmured into her ear. Her hair tickled my lips, and I blew lightly.

Julia seemed to shiver in my arms. I concentrated on teaching her the dance steps.

"Look," I said, holding her so she could feel my right thigh pushing against her. "Back a step, sway . . ." The side of her breast moved against my arm. "And turn." My voice had gone hoarse.

At the end of the number, Julia kept hold of my hand as we left the floor. "Let's get some punch," she said. "I'll bet it's cooler on the verandah."

A few minutes later, when I was kissing her in the darkness, I could taste the cool punch just on the inside of her lower lip.

Chapter Two

THE FEW STEPS down to Dad's barbershop felt like a change of climate. The air was cooler, a little dank and stuffy. The overhead fans made a peaceful clacking sound.

Shorty McHugh, the barber who worked for Dad, had somebody tipped back, his face under a warm towel. Whoever was under there looked relaxed enough to be asleep, his heels almost together and his toes drooping out in a V shape.

Dad's chair was empty. He was cleaning up the counter and had his back to the door. He looked at me in the mirror.

I was dressed up in an argyle vest and tie on account of the end-of-school assembly and the picnic at the park starting in just a little while.

"You got time?" I asked Dad.

He silently assessed my need for a haircut, which admittedly wasn't very great, but word was the Brown twins were taking pictures with their family's new home movie camera, and I might get into a few frames.

He swiveled the chair toward me. "Have a seat."

He fastened the strip of paper around my neck and flapped open the white cotton apron.

"Business good?" I asked.

"Mainly loafers until a while ago." He drew the comb through my hair.

I pulled the heavy smells of hair tonic mixed with shaving soap over me like a blanket and shut my eyes. But when I did that I thought of Julia.

I opened my eyes. Dad's clipping sent tufts of straw-colored hair into my lap. The gray and black snakelike pattern of the electrical cord twitched on my shoulder. The oil he used on the blades made a warm smell.

The chair next to me squeaked as Shorty set his customer up. The guy in the other chair—who I still couldn't see—sighed and murmured something, and then I heard little smacking sounds as Shorty patted shaving lotion on the man's face.

"That your boy in that chair, Sparky?" the man asked in a voice that sounded kinda familiar. People around town called Dad "Sparky" because he had a way with cars, understanding better than the average person about spark plugs and stuff.

Dad turned my chair so I was facing the customer.

Mr. Goodwin's sunset blond hair gleamed with hair tonic, and his ears appeared larger than usual. His skin was so clean shaven he looked babyish.

"Hello," I said, feeling my face turn red.

Mr. Goodwin smiled and nodded, making no reference to the fact that I'd been on his porch fairly often in the last few weeks.

"So where's that magazine you were telling me about?" he asked Dad as he slid his tie into place. "The one on auto camping. This it?" He held up a magazine from the pile Dad kept on a table by the ashtray and spittoon.

"Yep." Dad turned me around so I could see my haircut and he could talk to Mr. Goodwin in the mirror. "See how they fixed the front seat so it folds back to make a bed? I'm thinking about trying that."

Dad snipped automatically, chatting about auto tents and his plans to take us on a driving trip to see the West.

Mr. Goodwin closed the magazine. "My boy Paul would get a kick out of this auto camping. But I don't think the missus would go for it. She wouldn't like sleeping out in the open. Not my girl either."

My girl. He was talking about Julia.

"You gonna give that boy of yours a real barbershop shave?" Mr. Goodwin asked on his way out.

Dad seemed to notice me again, brushing a triangle of hair off my cheek. "You want a shave, son?" he asked as the door shut behind Mr. Goodwin.

I'd always used one of the safety razors we had at home.

Dad touched the gleaming straight razor that hung from a peg behind his chair. "I got the time if you have."

He and Shorty were both watching me.

I shrugged. "Sure."

Dad moved quickly, tipping me back until I was almost horizontal and placing a white towel over my front, keeping up a running conversation with Shorty about fishing while he stropped the razor. I stared mainly at the pressed-tin tiles on the ceiling, reminding myself that Dad did this every day.

He swirled up a foamy lather in the shaving mug and slathered it on my face. His eyes met mine, and the edge of the razor settled on my cheekbone.

It was nervous making. Not painful exactly, but a series of close, efficient scrapes that removed some of my surface. When Dad drew the razor under my jawline, I felt my pulse in my throat.

When he was done, he took a hot towel out of the steam cabinet. "Here's the good part," he said, placing it on my face, the damp, heavy heat jarring. Then the weight became soothing. Dad's fingers worked expertly, arranging the towel so I could breathe, yet covering every inch of my recently skinned face. It was like being tucked into bed. He put his hand on my shoulder for a second, then I sensed him move away.

As all the muscles in my body relaxed, my feet fell open into a V shape.

When I got to the picnic a half hour later, I saw Julia, leaning against a picnic table, talking to Rob Cummings in that way she had of staring at the ground as if considering what brilliant thing you'd said, then flashing her eyes up at you so fast and full of interest that you felt you'd been touched by God.

I wanted to push Rob's face in—though he was an okay guy when he wasn't hanging around Julia.

"Jim! Hey!" my friend Noah called.

He and some other kids were trying to suspend the blue and gold *Class of 1931* banner from the overhang of the gazebo. The juniors always raised the class banner for the seniors.

Noah stood on the railing on tiptoes, clinging to a post with one hand, stretching toward the gingerbread of the overhang with the other. "We need some height here," he said.

"Want me to try?"

He leapt to the ground and handed me the banner.

I threw it over my shoulder and climbed up to take his place on the railing. Was Julia watching? Since our first date, we'd gone out four times. No place important—once, we'd just walked her little brother to the library and waited on the steps until he was through looking up something in the *Encyclopedia Britannica*. But each time, we'd ended up in the darkness kissing until we were half crazy.

Yet I'd heard Julia had gone to the movies with Rob Cummings and to somebody's birthday party with one of the guys on the baseball team. And around school, she just treated me with the same sweet matter-of-factness she gave all her admirers. But I couldn't believe she did with everybody what she did with me. Otherwise, there'd be talk.

"You've about got it," Noah coached from the grass. "A couple of more inches and you're there."

I stretched until I felt my toes slipping on the railing and my shoulder separating from its socket. The tassel of the gold cord barely brushed the hole in the gingerbread. A tiny spider parachuted out a silvery thread, and a bead of sweat shot down my spine.

As I made the final reach, my trousers slipped below my waistline and my shirt came untucked. The breeze tickled my bare belly, and I hoped Julia wasn't watching after all.

I pulled the end of the cord through and raised the banner. A peppering of applause greeted me as I jumped down. Frank was pointing the celebrated home movie camera my way. Noah shook my hand as solemnly as if I had planted the American flag on a newly discovered island. I could hear the odd clicking sound of the camera, and then Frank turned it away from us.

On the other side of the gazebo somebody had cranked up a portable phonograph. The smell of a roasting pig donated by the Odd Fellows wavered in the air. I moved toward the group of kids that included Julia, but she and Rob were already headed my way, walking with a purpose.

They went right by me, Julia close enough that I could see the little spray of pale freckles on her cheek. She smiled as she passed. "Hi!"

"Hello."

Magnetized, I followed a few steps and then cut over to the lemonade table. I didn't want to watch her dance with Rob.

So why did I gulp down the lemonade, keeping a mouthful of ice, and go back? Why did I lean against the railing of the gazebo, crunching the bits of ice between my teeth as if they were Rob's bones, and watch?

Julia was using stuff I'd taught her—the little back step and weight shift, especially. What else was she using that I'd taught her? But I hadn't really taught her the other stuff. We'd learned it together.

I hated feeling this way.

The record ended, and she smiled at Rob and thanked him. Then she walked over to me. My insides went nuts, but

I wasn't going to let her see it, not while pigs had ears. I made myself meet her eyes casually.

"It's hot," she said, fanning her hand in front of her face.

"Yeah."

Julia wore a white dress printed with tiny sprigs of pale flowers.

"Look!" She pointed to where Frank now had his tripod set up by the Browns' fancy new Chevrolet Cabriolet. Couples were taking turns having their pictures made, the guys sitting behind the wheel of the green convertible as if they owned it.

Julia touched the ribbon that held her hair back. "Is my hair smooth?"

I nodded.

She brushed a fleck of something off my sleeve and then she took my hand. "Want to have Fred take our picture?"

I waited so long to answer that a little dip appeared between Julia's brows.

Our picture? I searched Julia's face to make sure. Then the giddiness set. What an incredible end to the school year.

"Sure!" I said.

Noah was one of the kids watching the filming, and I goofily punched him in the arm with my free hand as Julia and I stood beside him waiting our turn.

"I hear Mr. Brown paid over six hundred dollars for that heap," he said.

A senior sat behind the wheel of the gleaming auto-mobile, waving at the camera. His girlfriend and a gang of her buddies swarmed the car, lolling on the curved fenders.

When they were done, Flo Brown motioned to Julia. "Want to try it out?" she called.

We swung our linked hands casually as we walked to the car.

"You get behind the wheel," I said, opening the door for her.

"Why?"

"Because you *drive* me crazy," I whispered.

Julia laughed and slid in. I leaned on the door and smiled for the camera. And so Julia and I became an official couple and I began the summer in a state of bliss.

On a Saturday afternoon a few weeks after the end-of-school picnic, I arrived home from work to find an auto tent from Sears Roebuck partially set up in the yard. Dad's Model A Ford was parked in the shade, and all I could see of him were his long legs sticking out as he worked at something inside the car. Amos, unexpectedly home for the weekend, messed around under the hood. Cathy barely looked up from changing the clothes of the new doll that Amos had brought her last night.

Dad was over the moon about this trip to see the West. He'd piled the dining room table high with old motoring magazines, road maps, and lists. And Mama was thrilled because she'd be sending back a series of articles on the American West to the *Jefferson Herald*, and getting her very own byline. I didn't want to go, because the minute I left town Julia would be up for grabs.

Inside, I changed out of the starched white shirt I wore to work and went over my arguments for staying behind. I had a job. I could look after the house for the weeks they'd be gone. If I really needed anything, Amos was just forty miles away at school.

As I went back downstairs, I saw Mama's bedroom door still closed. She'd been lying down when I got home from work last night, and she hadn't even stirred to say hello to Amos when he'd showed up about eight thirty. She probably had one of her sick headaches.

When I got outside, Dad was cleaning dark streaks off his hands with a gasoline-soaked rag.

"Want me to finish setting up the tent?" I asked. "Just to make sure it works?"

"That'd be all right," he said, without really meeting my eyes.

I knelt by the pile of canvas. The ground was still a little soft from the heavy rain the night before, and my knees got damp as I threaded rope through grommets.

Amos came over and picked up one corner of the canvas, aligning two edges. "What's wrong with Dad?" I asked.

He shrugged. "Maybe he and Mama are having a fight about something."

"I've been thinking about not going on the trip," I said, expecting him to be shocked that I'd miss the grand tour of the West.

To my surprise, he said, "That's not a bad idea. You could take care of things around here. Check in on Shorty down at the barbershop and make sure it's running right. Keep your job. Jobs aren't a dime a dozen anymore."

My brother was on my side.

The warped screen door thumped, and Mama came out, her arms folded across her chest as if she were chilled. Cathy picked up the new doll and went to show Mama, who barely glanced at it. Dad ignored all of us, staying half buried inside the car.

Amos lowered his voice. "The folks may not be gone all that long anyway. I don't think Dad has any idea what it's like out there. A few years back, these car trips were just grand. But things are changing. The other day, I heard—"

He broke off as Mama drifted over. Her eyes were swollen.

Cathy leaned against my side. "My new dolly is going to ride in the car with me. I'll show her the grand vistas," she said, using an expression she'd been hearing from Mama ten times a day.

Cathy wouldn't know a grand vista from a prairie dog, but she'd be okay without me for a few weeks. Right there in the car, they'd have to pay attention to her.

Dad joined us, his gaze not rising above Mama's kneecaps.

"Tell them," she demanded, her voice sounding like she had a terrible cold.

Tell us what? I was suddenly aware of Cathy's heartbeat against the side of my arm. I glanced at Amos.

"I sold the barbershop," Dad said.

The taffeta dress of the doll rustled as Cathy shifted her from one arm to the other.

Sold the barbershop? What would we do for money?

"How can you be thinking of a tour of the West if you don't even have employment?" Amos demanded.

"We're selling the place, too," Dad said, making a gesture toward the house. "Moving to Colorado," he concluded, as if glad to have the news finally over with.

"What?" I yelped. I jumped up, sending Cathy sprawling in the grass. "I'm not moving to Colorado!"

Amos got to his feet, too. "That's just nuts, Dad. Don't you know about the farmers having trouble growing things? The land's not producing."

Dad was taller than both Amos and me. "But people always need to eat, son. That's why we'll open a grocery store."

Then I remembered the grocery-store conversation from weeks ago. Dad wanted to be a grocer in Colorado instead of a barber in Iowa.

"But, Dad, a lot of people can't even afford to buy food. Haven't you heard about the breadlines and soup kitchens?" Amos demanded, glancing at Mama for support.

Her tear-swollen eyes were angry, but I could tell by the way she hugged herself that Dad was going to win.

"Son, haven't *you* heard prosperity is just around the corner? That's what President Hoover says."

And President Hoover was one of our own—born a hundred and fifty or so miles east.

"They call the shantytowns that are popping up *Hoovervilles*," Amos snapped. He did an about-face and strode over to the car, lowering the hood with a clanging bang, then just standing there with his hands on the hood.

Dad had a look around his mouth I didn't see very often. But it was deep set and dug in. He had sold his livelihood and our home. There was no turning back.

Cathy leaned against my legs.

Over the next couple of weeks, Dad treated my plan to stay behind with a forced casualness—which was how he treated everything involved with the move. I truly hoped he knew what he was doing. Or, if he didn't, that the fates would be kind and still let his adventure turn out okay.

My staying didn't seem to make much of an impression on Mama one way or the other. Around home, she was distracted, losing track of things—putting a skillet in the auction pile, then needing it to make supper—donating her favorite novel to the library, then having to call and ask for it back. But in public, she stood loyally beside Dad, doing the best she could to face down the talk about the foolishness of his pulling up stakes at such a time.

Cathy played with her dolls in the new cubbyholes formed by boxes and shifted furniture. Eventually, the new doll took on the same raggedness as Cathy herself.

Noah's family had said I could stay with them if I'd pay a little room and board while I finished my last year of high school. And by then, Amos would be graduated from college and we could make more permanent plans.

Julia blushed when the subject of my family's move came up, like she was sort of embarrassed about the whole thing. But she whispered, "I'm so glad you're staying!" between our salty, sweet kisses.

I wasn't taking much over to Noah's—mainly my clothing, shaving kit, and books. And my typewriter. And my bedding, which Noah's mom had asked me to bring.

I was in my room rolling up my sheet and blanket when Cathy came skipping in. "Let me help you pack," she said.

I straddled the bedroll and cast a piece of cord around it.

She took the two ends. "I can tie the bow. Watch."

Mama banged cupboard doors downstairs, checking for missed things.

"You're not watching," Cathy said, her eyes on mine.

Mama's footsteps resounded off the bare floor, against the uncurtained windows, and through the empty rooms. I'd been conceived and born in this house.

Cathy threw down the ends of the cord in frustration. Her bow had only one loop instead of two. "It's wrong," she said.

I pressed the bedroll more tightly, giving her some slack in the cord. "Now try."

Through the open window, I could hear Dad outside talking to somebody. A few unsold things still sat on the front porch, including the icebox, which Mrs. Harker next door was buying. In the drive, the car had a load strapped on top. Julia said it looked like the Model A was wearing a hat. She'd be here soon to help me take my stuff over to Noah's.

"There!" Cathy sat back, drawing the bow tight and folding her hands in her lap, waiting for my approval.

"Good." She had a tiny dark speck on the side of her neck, right below her ear. I drew her to the window so I could see better. It could be a tick, the way Cathy was always playing tea party under bushes. Would Mama remember to check Cathy for ticks?

I pushed the worry away when I heard Julia's voice in the yard. "Up here!" I waved from the window.

Julia, who'd been looking at the car, turned and waved back.

Cathy stood beside me. "It'll be fun sleeping in the car."

"There should be just enough room for you and two dollies," I said, squatting down to look at her neck again. In the bright light, I saw it was just a fleck of leaf or dirt. I rubbed it off.

"There'll be room for you, too, silly!'

"But, Cathy—"

The look in her eyes made the shocking announcement to me that she didn't know. She hadn't been listening, and I hadn't been paying enough attention to her to realize she thought I was going with them.

I had been charging along to a castle on the horizon, where no dragon guarded the princess.

"Cathy," I whispered. "I'm not . . ."

Mama's litany when Cathy was a baby with heavy, smelly diapers had been "Jim's such a good boy. He loves his little sister so."

I fixed my gaze on the castle with the sun rising behind it. Cathy wasn't my responsibility.

When I was twelve, I'd run home after school hungry to see Cathy—barely old enough to pull herself up at the screen door—waiting for me.

Now the screen door opened and closed behind Julia.

Cathy's eyes looked just a little puzzled, still innocent of my betrayal.

Julia's clothing rustled with a silky rhythm as she ran up the stairs.

When I finished my sentence—*I'm not going*—something inside Cathy would be changed forever. It would be a killing.

I shut my eyes. I didn't want to see it.

"Jim," Julia exclaimed. "There you are."

Chapter Three

CATHY SAT UP. Wrinkles from my trousers were printed on the side of her face like lines on a road map, and the place where her head had rested in my lap felt warm and a little damp.

We were somewhere in the middle of Nebraska, driving for what seemed to be the rest of time along the shallow, wide Platte River.

Cathy pointed out the window at the flocks of long-legged, gray birds wading in the water. "Jim, look!"

"Sandhill cranes," I explained, shifting and stretching my legs.

Julia's letter made a bulge in my left pocket. I'd tried to tell her how sorry I was that I had to go with my family after all. I'd followed her right up onto her porch, wanting to take her hand for a minute or have her really look at me. But just as though she'd already erased me, she walked through her front door and let it swing closed in my face.

Her little brother, Paul, playing with his toy soldiers on the porch, had clutched his heart, gurgled, fallen, twitched once, and died.

The morning we'd left, I'd found Julia's letter wedged in the screen door. *I gave myself to you. . . . You meant everything to me. . . . I never want to hear from you again. . . .*

I'd been trying to write an answer across Iowa and half of Nebraska. I'd filled six sheets of paper and part of a seventh so far.

"We'll make camp here," Dad said, nosing the car down a little embankment on the left and driving through grass toward the river.

They said the Platte was a mile wide and a foot deep, and it looked it—sandbars dotted the surface. A flock of cranes took to the air just long enough to settle down on the other side of some scrub bushes growing in the middle of the river.

There were no trees to camp under, but I got out of the car, grateful to be standing upright. The prairie had disappeared around Kearney, so now we had only the river and the plains covered with green blankets of new corn.

What would Amos think of so much corn?

We'd been on the road for six days, making a side trip to see one of Dad's cousins north of Grand Island. Sometimes we'd sailed along on concrete at thirty miles an hour. Other times we bounced over graveled highways until I thought the wheels would fall off. We'd had a breakdown outside a little town called Silver Creek, and I'd handed Dad tools and held parts until he got the car running again.

Did it bother him that where we were headed, nobody would know his nickname—Sparky?

He untangled his fishing pole from our camping supplies and started toward the river. "Maybe I can catch our supper."

"I'm getting tired of fried bologna," Mama said to his back.

She got out the camping stove and I set up the canvas stools. Then I started unpacking the tent.

"Can we go wading?" Cathy asked, tugging on my hand.

Down by the river, we put our shoes and socks on a rock. I rolled up my trousers and knotted my sister's skirt so it made a bubble below her waist, leaving her thin legs bare.

"Don't fly off with the cranes," I told her.

She took one step into the current; her eyes widened and she grabbed my hand. Together, we eased along. I felt gritty sand and little stems of plants beneath my feet. The river breathed out a steady whooshing sound. The dropping sun made the water gleam as if it were carrying particles of gold. I tried to conjure Julia, but she was six days away, and tomorrow would be seven.

"I wish we had a boat to sail," Cathy said after we'd waded for half an hour or so.

In the distance, Dad held out a string of fish to Mama. From where we stood, my parents looked no bigger than the pair of cranes fishing a hundred yards away from Cathy and me.

"I guess we could make a boat," I said.

I led her back onto the grass, and we sat down. Taking the last page of my letter to Julia—the page that had only five words on it, which I could always write again—I folded it lengthwise, creasing it against my knee. Then I folded that in half the other way, opened it, and brought the corners in to make a triangle. I rolled back the flaps and shaped it into a little tub of a boat.

Cathy cried, "Magic!" as she grabbed it and raced to the water.

I followed, standing beside her and watching the white shape spin in the gold water, catch on a finger of river grass, then sail steadily on for several feet. Cathy clapped and danced, running along beside it. The paper became water-logged eventually, and the boat capsized, rolled on its side, and drifted. Finally, it sank.

"Do it again!" Cathy demanded, grabbing my hands with her wet ones.

So I folded up another piece of my letter to Julia, the ink turning to watercolor under my damp fingers.

Some of our boats sailed farther than others. When I was down to my last two pieces of paper, I folded them quickly and helped Cathy send them off as a pair. They were still floating when I pulled her away from the river.

"I need to set up the tent," I said. "The sun's going down."

"Dad's fish smells good," Cathy said. "I'm hungry."

"Me, too."

After North Platte, we arced southwest into Colorado. The roads were rough, and a day of rain had turned innocent dips into sucking mud holes.

Twice we'd gotten stuck. Pestered by evil-tempered flies, Dad and I took turns carrying a tow rope to the far side and waiting for somebody to come along and pull us out. The people who helped us then drove on into the mire, stalling as well. Eventually, I guess, somebody came from the other direction and pulled them out.

"I don't feel good," Cathy murmured from the seat beside me. Her lips were pale and she held her fist knotted over her stomach.

The water in the cabin camp where we'd stayed last night had tasted strange. Yet it had a funny way of making a person want more, and I'd found myself gulping it.

Folks at the camp had been talking about how the hard times were turning people desperate and angry and how the country was in danger from the anarchists and the Reds.

A man in a battered, dusty truck camped next to us told Dad, "You folks better turn around and go back home." He talked about things he'd seen in the Oklahoma panhandle, and just shook his head at Dad's idea of finding a good place to open a grocery store. "Take my advice and go home," he'd repeated.

Maybe that was what had kept me awake all night. That and the people camped close to us, making their own smells and sounds. And the look on Mama's face as she'd focused on what the man was saying.

As we continued our drive west that morning, Mama and Dad were arguing in the front seat and paying no attention to Cathy's stomachache.

"Want me to read to you?" I asked.

She nodded.

The edges of the book's pale green cover were worn where hands had held it open. Last night, a woman had come over to our campfire just as we were bedding down and offered the book to Cathy. Cathy had taken it shyly, one hand clutching my shirtsleeve. Then the woman had backed away into the darkness, her husband tugging on her arm.

And that was another thing I'd wondered about in the night. If the book belonged to the woman's little girl, why didn't she need it anymore?

"Who killed Cock Robin?" I began, having to stop to yawn. "'I,' said the sparrow. 'With my bow and arrow. I killed Cock Robin.'"

Back home, just inside the front door, in an oval frame, we'd had a picture of a little girl gazing at a robin. That picture had hung there as long as I could remember. I swallowed, my mouth dry—but I didn't want to drink any more of the water we'd carried from the campground.

Cathy was looking up at me, the shape of her pale eyebrows showing her confusion. I wished the lady had given my little sister a more cheerful storybook.

"What does that page say?" she asked, pointing.

"Who saw him die? 'I,' said the fly. 'With my little eye, I saw him die.'"

"Why is he dead?" Cathy asked after a beat.

"Because the sparrow shot him."

"*Why?*" Puzzlement and horror wrinkled the word.

How should I know? For no reason at all, probably.

I smacked the book shut. There were a lot of *why*s I didn't know the answer to, all of them more important than a dead bird and a talking insect, and I was so tired I could hardly see.

Tears began to roll down Cathy's cheek as she cried silently, staring at her muddy shoes.

I wanted to kick the seat in front of me. I wanted to run screaming across the plains away from this stinking, rattling box that I had been in so long I'd forgotten important things like what flavors of ice cream we served at the Cottage and where the apostrophe key was on the typewriter. I shut my eyes and clenched my teeth.

Pretty soon, Cathy curled up and laid her head in my lap, and her forgiveness made me feel like bawling, too.

Dad had to be stupid, Mama was saying, not to heed the signs. It wasn't too late. They could still go back.

Smoke from Dad's cigarette raked my face. Without opening my eyes, I could imagine its tip glowing angrily red.

In a voice dripping with reason, he said, "Mona, this won't work if you don't come up with a better attitude."

There was a sudden thumping noise, and I thought for a moment that Mama had actually hit him. But the end of a rope used to tie our possessions on top of the car had come loose and begun to bang against the side door as we rocked over the potholes.

"You're blaming me if this fails? Did you listen when I said we should stay put where we belong?"

"Mona, if you would just—" Dad began.

With a lurch, we went onto paved road, the first patch in a long time. The tires made a singing sound as Dad picked up speed.

"Well, thank God for that at least," Mama muttered.

They argued all the way through Sterling, which might have been a good place to stop and inquire about grocery stores, but Dad seemed to have forgotten what we were here for. He just wanted Mama to know he wasn't going back.

"I hate that damned barbershop," he said, grinding the gears. "And we don't have it anymore anyway, so quit yapping about it."

"And we don't have a place to live or a stick of furniture to call our own," she shot back.

I tried to concentrate on the rope's erratic tapping rather than their fighting. I told myself that Dad had always taken care of us somehow. Yet I remembered Mama's explanation to me one night not long before we left that when men reached a certain age, sometimes they did crazy, unsettling things.

The sun bored into the car. The end of a loaf of bread we'd bought back in North Platte began to give off an aroma like it was just being baked. My muddy shoes rested on a roll of dirty socks and underwear wrapped inside one of Dad's soiled shirts.

I hadn't shaved in a long time. Dad's face was as good as a mirror, so I knew what I looked like. I rubbed my jaw, remembering the barbershop shave, the press of hot towels on my face, the *cleanness* of everything.

The argument in the front finally ran down. Cathy fell asleep, her eyelids twitching. I yawned and folded a towel between my head and the window.

⌒✺⌒

Sometimes I thought I wasn't sleeping at all. I rocked and bounced around in hot air and car movements. Other times, I dropped into holes of sleep so deep the world could have ended and I would have missed it. I floated up to the surface, then sank back down.

What sensory alarm finally yanked me awake? How did I come to realize that Cathy's head was no longer in my lap? That she was no longer in the seat beside me?

I lurched forward to peer between Dad and Mama.

Mama jumped. "What?"

Dad glanced at me in the rearview mirror.

"Where's Cathy?" The words seemed to come out slowly, to stretch out like taffy pulled so fine it finally breaks.

"What?" Mama breathed, turning around. "Isn't she back there with you?"

Dad hit his brakes.

I yanked up the towel and piles of clothes, searching. Stupid. Not knowing what I was doing. "I was asleep—"

Dad pulled to the side of the road and jumped out.

The last place I remembered clearly was Sterling, but that was miles back.

For some reason, Dad was running around the car.

"Where are we?" I shook Mama, who had gone rigid and pale.

"Oh no," Dad groaned, piling back in the car.

"When we stopped for gasoline—" Mama began.

"Briggsdale," Dad said.

"I'll bet she got out," Mama said. "Didn't you notice?" she asked me.

Dad shot her a look.

How could I have slept through a gasoline stop? Had Cathy tried to wake me? Maybe she had. Maybe there was something in my dreams about somebody trying to wake me up.

I scrubbed the heels of my hands against my eyes, praying I was still asleep. But the sun beat down on endless acres of empty grassland. I would never dream this.

"Why wasn't anybody paying attention?" I yelled. "How could you lose Cathy?"

Dad muttered something as he reversed, backing into the ditch, the tall grass dragging against the chassis. Then we lurched onto the road.

Something happened.

I pitched forward, banging my face on the back of the front seat. Dad cussed and Mama screamed.

The motor had died, leaving a silence in which I heard the left front wheel wobbling along until it finally fell over in the ditch.

I tasted blood.

"*William*—" Mama gasped in pain.

Dad opened the door and half tumbled out of the car. He turned to help Mama, who was cradling her left wrist like a baby to her breast.

I leaned my forehead against the rear of the front seat, exploring the inside of my mouth with my tongue, feeling the sharp sting of the cut.

"You all right?" Dad asked, opening my door.

I nodded, licking my lips.

"Wheel came off," he said.

Of course the stupid wheel came off. It was a wonder they hadn't all come off, with the roads we'd been driving on for days.

"Where's Cathy?" I asked, disgust and a fat lip thickening my words. "Where'd you leave her?"

Dad's head reacted to the blow of my accusation as if I'd swung at him. "We just stopped once," he said. "A town called Briggsdale, for gas. Maybe three or four miles back. She'll be okay."

How did he know she'd be okay? He hadn't even known she was gone. I tried to get my balance.

The left front end of the car was resting on the axle, making the fender the height of a bench. Mama sat on it, still cradling her wrist. Earlier, she'd rolled down her stockings in the heat. The garters and fabric made little inner tubes around her ankles.

Birds sang from the grass. The engine ticked as it

cooled. I turned, surveying the hills. There wasn't a sign of civilization except for the ribbon of gravel that disappeared over the hilltop.

Somebody would come along eventually.

I saw Cathy's face. Her irregularly shaped baby teeth.

I started walking back the way we'd come. Chunks of gravel shifted under my feet, rattling in the silence.

"Where are you going?" Dad called.

"Back to find Cathy," I answered, without turning around.

"Jim!" Dad's voice said I owed him the respect of speaking to him directly.

I turned around, but I didn't owe him anything. This was all his fault. I'd still have my home, my job, my friends, my typewriter, and my girlfriend if Dad hadn't decided *he* needed a change.

"I'll find her while you take care of things here. And Mama." She was as hopeless as Dad about Cathy, but this trip hadn't been her idea. Her wrist was broken, for all I knew.

I couldn't see Dad's expression beneath the shadow of his straw hat.

"When you find her, you wait there," he finally instructed me.

"Yeah." I started walking again. Pale blue flowers, the color of Cathy's eyes, grew beside the road.

"It was a gas station on this side of town," Dad called. "A Texaco. And send somebody back to help us. I can't fix this much damage by myself."

As soon as I was over the crest of the hill, I started to run. The momentum carried me about halfway up the next hill before I had to slow down.

What had Cathy done when she realized we'd left her? Had she stayed at the gas station? Was someone looking after her?

I forced myself to stick to a scouts' pace. Walk fifty. Run fifty. If I could keep that up, I'd be back to town in less than an hour.

Chapter Four

UNDER THE NOONDAY SUN, the grass gave off a toasty, sweet smell. The silence was huge. My breathing, my shoes on the gravel, my shirt rubbing against itself as I pumped my arms seemed startling.

And then I heard the car coming up over the hill. It putted to a stop beside me. A dusty old Model T.

The driver was about Amos's age. "You belong to the folks back there?"

I nodded. My mouth was so dry, I didn't know if I could form words.

"They said I should take you to the Texaco station," he said. "That sound all right?"

"Yeah," I managed. "Thanks." I got in the car. I guess they hadn't told him about losing Cathy, or he'd surely mention it.

"Where you from?" he asked as we rattled along.

From the top of a hill, I saw the water tower of Briggs-dale in the distance. I was going east again. Toward water. I could drink and drink and drink.

"Iowa." To my horror, saying the word made my eyes go wet.

"I never been to *I-o-way*." He pronounced it like a lot of people from someplace else. "But I been to Enid, Oklahoma, to get my sister and her young 'uns last month. The trip made me glad to get home."

A sound almost escaped. *Home.* God, what was happening to me? I'd been fine when I was running half mad with fear that I'd never get to Cathy. Now that we were coming into town and I saw the Texaco right where Dad said it would be, I felt like bawling.

"Ned Thompson here can send somebody back to help your folks," the guy was saying, but I was already out of the car.

"Thanks," I called, waving without turning around.

I saw Cathy through the window. She had something in her hand and faced away from me.

"Hey," I said, going through the door.

She whirled. "Jim!"

She dropped a dripping pink ice cream cone and threw herself at me, clinging. I caught the odor of vomit beneath the sugary strawberry smell. The familiar feel of her made my head go light.

"You know this guy, honey?" a woman on the phone asked, but she was smiling. Cathy didn't answer, but she had her arms around my neck like a constrictor. "I guess you do," the woman said. Then she told the person on the other end of the line that the problem was solved. The little girl's family was here.

"Sorry about the mess," I said. The ice cream smeared the counter and puddled on the floor. "We'll clean it up."

"You don't need to do that," she said, looking me over. She probably thought I was an Okie—unshaven, a fat lip, blood in my beard, ragtag, with a stinky little sister lost beside the road.

I wanted her to know I was the son of a shop owner who had lived in a nice house back in Jefferson, Iowa, who had a typewriter and aspirations to be a journalist. I wanted her to know the prettiest, most popular girl in school picked me to be her boyfriend.

"Thanks for taking care of her," I said. "My folks lost a wheel off our car about four miles west of town. Could you send somebody?"

We arranged for her husband to go out and take another guy with him. I said I'd wait here with Cathy so we could at least be in the shade.

We sat under a cottonwood tree at the side of the gas station for a while. I got us two bottles of grape pop out of the cooler, but I had to kind of pour it in my mouth because of my swollen lip.

"What happened to you?" Cathy asked, touching my face.

"I connected with a seat back," I said. "What happened to you? Where'd you *go*?"

"When we stopped, I got sick. I ran around the side of the building to throw up."

"Why didn't you wake me?"

"I was in a hurry."

A familiar car pulled in for gas, and the guy who'd given me the lift got out. "Hey, who's your friend?" he called.

"My little sister. What are you doing back here?"

"Aw, I gotta go on to Sterling. They don't have the part we need at the hardware store. Gonna get gas before I set out."

I was about four miles closer to home than I'd been an hour ago. Sterling would be fifty miles closer yet. The pull of Iowa was so strong it made my jaws ache.

"Any chance we could get a lift?" I asked, nodding at Cathy.

He hesitated, probably wondering where Cathy had popped up from and why we were now headed in the opposite direction from our folks. Finally he shrugged. "Sure. Just let me fill her up."

I took Cathy into the bathroom and washed her face, hands, and arms with cold water and a small piece of green soap. I was among strangers in a place I'd never see again in my life. Dad and Mama and Amos weren't around to tell me what to do. Well, Dad had told me what to do, but it didn't seem right. Mama could have given me good advice once, but she almost seemed to be having a kind of breakdown.

By the time I'd splashed a lot of water on my face, drinking half of it, I'd made up my mind. I'd seen a train station in Sterling, and I had money from working at the Cottage.

I wiped my face on the jammed towel roll that was damp from other people. Then I went around front and asked the lady who'd taken care of Cathy if she had a piece of paper for me to write a note on. Without letting myself think, I scribbled *Getting a train in Sterling to go home. Amos and I can work things out. Cathy's okay. Hope Mama's wrist isn't broken. Jim.*

I folded it, wrote **William Snow** on the front, and handed it to the woman. "Would you give this to my folks when they get here?"

I took Cathy's hand and led her to the guy's car.

"You ready?" he asked.

"Yeah," I said. "I'm ready."

The next morning, the stationmaster, in a fresh uniform and cleanly shaven, slid numbers into slots on the arrival/departure board. Our train was due at eight forty.

A Western Union guy tapped out Morse code behind the window.

Cathy scuffed one shoe against the other and yawned deeply.

Four clocks hung on the back wall—one for each time zone. It was eight fifteen, Mountain Time, and I held Dad's single-word telegram in my hand. *Wait.*

A team and wagon stopped in front of the station. The animals stamped, jingling their harnesses, and the smell of fresh horse apples drifted through the open door.

Cathy began to scoot forward and backward on the bench, each time going nearer to the edge.

"I spy something with two hands," I said to distract her. I stared at the clocks. Should I wait or not?

"Is it that man there?" Cathy whispered. "He has two hands."

She gazed at the shabby man just coming through the door. I was pretty sure he was a hobo. I'd heard them in the night, getting off the last train, talking in the shadows. It had turned cold after the sun went down, and one of them had a hacking cough.

Before the stationmaster had gone home for supper, he'd given Cathy and me blankets when he figured out we had no place to wait the night except the train station.

Cathy lost interest in I Spy. "Where's Daddy and Mama?"

"I'll bet they're getting the car fixed," I told her, making my voice cheerful, as if it were the most natural thing in the world that we'd slept all night huddled on a bench and were headed home without our parents. And home wasn't even there anymore—though Cathy might not understand that.

I unfolded the telegram. *Wait.* I folded it back up.

I'd got us this far, and I had two train tickets in my pocket. Right or wrong, whatever I did, the world seemed to keep wobbling around on its axis.

Dad and Mama would be mad no matter what I did. Mad I'd started for home. Mad whether I waited or not.

"Spare a dime?" the tramp asked quietly. His face had the dry rash of fever. He crooked his elbow over his face to muffle his cough.

Had Mama gone to a doctor about her wrist?

I found two nickels in my pocket and handed them to him. Cathy put her head in my lap and I stared at the clocks.

Eight twenty-five. Nine twenty-five at home.

When Dad and Mama came through the door, I had the sense that Mama was supporting Dad, despite the triangle of fabric that held her left arm in a sling.

Cathy stirred against my side and sat up, smiling. "Did you get the car fixed?"

"It's fixed," Dad said.

I stared ahead, at first not looking at Dad. Then, when I finally met his eyes, he glanced away.

Mama touched Cathy's hair and then sank down on the bench beside us. Dad kept standing.

"Does your arm hurt?" Cathy asked Mama.

"A little bit."

Neither of my parents spoke to me. I shut my eyes, still seeing the afterimage of their silhouettes in the doorway. A blanket of dancing speckles erased the image, and I was so tired I just left my eyes closed.

"What are we going to do?" Mama asked after a minute.

I opened my eyes. She looked worn-out and old. Pain scratched lines around her mouth. Was she talking to me?

"I'm going home," I said, sitting up and meeting her gaze. I slid my hand in my pocket, touching the two tickets.

"But you won't have a place to live," Mama said to me.

Weariness was making me giddy. I just shrugged.

Dad cleared his throat. When he spoke, he sounded like an amateur actor butchering his lines. "I still think we could make a go of it. We just need to find a good spot to settle down."

My body ached with tension and from having slept all night on a hard bench. My cut lip hurt. But the worst pain was from Dad's humiliation.

I lied, hoping my voice didn't sound as unconvincing as Dad's. "Probably can." I swallowed and took hold of Cathy's hand. "But I'm sixteen. I don't want to live in Colorado."

Mama acted like she had just heard an interesting idea and was giving it thoughtful consideration. "Going back is best," she decided, her voice gentle. "Things didn't turn out the way we thought they would." She used *we* generously, as if we had all decided on a plan that had looked good and reasonable at the time but to our astonishment had turned out to be folly.

Dad cleared his throat again.

I heard the whistle of the train coming in, and the urgency gave me energy. No matter what Dad and Mama did, I was getting on that train and taking Cathy with me. We'd be home in a couple of days. I'd make some kind of plan on the way. Maybe I'd send Amos a telegram, letting him know we were coming.

I stood, the movement stirring up my body odor. "What I wouldn't give for a haircut, a bath, and a shave," I muttered, and then regretted the words immediately when I saw the look on Dad's face.

The barbershop wasn't his anymore even if he did go back. What a mess.

"We can tell people we just got homesick," Mama said with a little laugh. She sat up straight with perky composure. "Surely anybody can understand that."

So was Mama coming with Cathy and me, without Dad? Would he let her do that? I looked from one to the other. What would it be like to be married? To be bound to another person, to not be able to move without them, like somebody in a perpetual three-legged race?

"The eight forty's arriving, folks," the stationmaster announced.

People with valises and bundles gathered them up and moved toward the door. Cathy held on to my hand with purpose, but when she looked from Mama to Dad and up at me, her eyes were uneasy. How could she understand it if I couldn't?

Dad spoke. "We could head toward home—"

I watched the battle on his face and wished we could just return to the month of May and start our lives over. Stop time and back up.

"—and on the way we could keep our eyes open for any good opportunity."

Mama nodded. "Yes," she said. "Maybe we missed something the first time. We can look again. And if we don't find anything, well . . ." She shrugged.

"This way, folks," the stationmaster called from the door, motioning to me.

I started toward him.

"Wait, Jim," Mama said, putting her hand on my arm. "Why don't you turn your tickets in? We can drive east. We'll start right now, won't we, William?"

Dad nodded, staring at the floor. Then he turned toward the door. We let him get ahead, so we appeared to be following his lead. He lifted his head and squared his shoulders. You had to know him well to see he looked like a man walking to his own hanging.

After I cashed in our tickets, I climbed in the back seat, Cathy beside me.

The morning sun was in our faces as we headed east from Sterling. Cathy held her book of nursery rhymes, but she didn't show any interest in reading it.

I leaned down and whispered in her ear. "Do not get out of the car without me. Okay?"

She nodded.

Even though I was exhausted, I started to think about practical things. Was there any chance I could get my old job back? What would I say to people when they asked why we returned so soon?

Cathy found her dolls in the jumble of the back seat and began to rock them.

It would be strange to drive by our house, to see Mrs. Harker hanging out diapers in her yard, and to know we couldn't go back.

Noah would have my typewriter and books. Maybe I could still stay with him, until we got settled into wherever we were going to live.

And, of course, there was one thing I didn't dare think about, so I kept thinking about not thinking about it. Julia.

Cathy
1942

Chapter One

I STOPPED BY the newspaper office Saturday afternoons. Each time, I saw my brother's name on the front window—James W. Snow, Assistant Editor—and knew people were reading what he had to say about victory gardens, the Battle of the Coral Sea, or the draft board. I nearly floated away with pride.

Today the vibration from the press made the window panes sing. "Jim?" I called.

"Back here, Cathy."

I heard Jim and Julia in conversation with somebody else in the file room.

"Hi," Paul Goodwin said, standing up.

Paul was my sister-in-law's brother—which I guess made him my brother-in-law by marriage or some such thing. I'd known him practically my whole life—not only because Jim and Julia were married, but because Amos was in a seed-corn development business with Mr. Goodwin. Paul had been away at college in the East for the last few years, coming home just for a little while each summer.

I greeted him with a wave.

"Paul enlisted," Jim explained.

"So I'm home until I start basic training next month," Paul told me. "What's new with you these days?"

I felt my face turning pink. "Nothing, really." Julia had on a suit I hadn't seen before with a peplum and narrow belt that set off her figure. "That's a pretty suit," I said, shifting the attention to her.

"Thank you." She turned, showing me the back. Then she said to Jim, "Are you about ready? We're supposed to meet the Wrights at the golf club at five."

"But I'd hoped you could drive Mary Ann and me out to Spring Lake." My best friend, Mary Ann, and I had been giving each other pep talks that there was more to life than paging through the Sears Roebuck catalogue looking at lingerie, lamps, and layettes and *dreaming* about our future. We needed to start living a little.

"*I* was thinking about going out to Spring Lake," Paul said. "Blue Barron's orchestra is playing tonight."

Julia smiled, opening her hands at the perfect solution. "Then *you* could chauffeur the girls."

Oh no. Mary Ann and I had never been to a Saturday night dance at Spring Lake. We were babies compared to a college boy. It would be excruciating. I turned to Jim for rescue, but he was caught up in conversation with Julia about something else.

Paul was looking a little uncomfortable, too. Did he already regret his offer?

"What time should I pick up you and your friend?" he asked.

Trying to get out of it now would seem hopelessly rude. "How about seven thirty?"

When I was on the sidewalk, back in the May sunshine, I shook my head. Mary Ann was going to kill me.

"That was *fun*," Mary Ann said, buttoning her jacket as we left the dance hall.

The reflections of the crystal ball that spun over the dance floor flickered through the windows.

"Cathy, you forgot your sweater," Paul called, catching up to me.

"Thanks." I pulled it around my shoulders.

I'd danced a lot more than I thought I would, because Paul had been polite and asked me several times.

His car was parked down by the lake. He led the way, the collar of his white shirt glowing in the dark. As we got farther from the music, the water made little tapping sounds against the swimming dock, where we'd be cooling off in a couple of months.

"I'll miss coming out here this summer," Paul remarked.

I didn't know what to say. *We'll miss you, too?* No, that sounded too stiff. *I'll bet you don't want to go off and fight in the war?* That sounded too stupid. My silence made me feel clumsy as I slid into the middle of the front seat.

"That was really fun," Mary Ann said again.

So much for scintillating conversation. Paul must think we were kids. I could hardly wait to get home and call Mary Ann and rehash the details of the evening without an audience.

"I'll drop Mary Ann off first," Paul said.

What would I say to Paul alone in the car? I hoped my nerves stirred up only my perfume and that I didn't smell sweaty.

He turned on the radio and spun the dial to WHO 1040. The *Iowa Barn Dance Frolic* broadcast from the Shrine Auditorium in Des Moines came in.

"Listen to those little feet go!" The sounds of tap dancing along with "The Yellow Rose of Texas" filled the car.

"How corny," Mary Ann murmured. "*Listening* to tap dancing."

At the end of the song, whoops came from the audience, and I had an image of proud little girls in yellow blouses and cowgirl hats curtsying. I snuck a look at Paul. Didn't college boys from the East have more sophisticated tastes?

Then Jerry and Zelda, who were on every week, sang "Tumbling Tumbleweed." Paul turned the volume low. "Dad says we have a new advertisement coming on tonight," he explained. "I want to hear it."

"For Amos's and Mr. Goodwin's seed corn," I explained to Mary Ann. We were almost to her house by then. "I'll call you," I whispered as she got out of the car.

Paul waited until she disappeared through her front door, then he backed out of the driveway. Zelda was saying, "And now a word from one of our favorite sponsors, G&S Seeds."

Paul turned up the volume as an announcer read the ad. "Farmers, you really should try G&S seeds." *G* was for Goodwin. *S* was for Snow. "If you're not using G&S yet, you should go out and get some and plant the G&S seeds right alongside those others you've been using. You'll see the difference by harvest time. And it'll be a difference you'll like."

Then Paul switched the dial to WGN in Chicago and we listened to Glenn Miller's recording of "American Patrol" the rest of the way to my house.

"Who all did you dance with tonight besides me? Anybody special?" he asked.

It sounded almost like he was fishing for information. Why would he care?

"Just boys," I said, feeling my face go hot in the darkness.

When we stopped in front of the little place we rented, I could see Mama through the window, reading.

"Wait," Paul said. "I'll get the door for you."

He hadn't opened the car door for Mary Ann, but he probably felt Jim and Julia had put him in official charge of me.

"I'll walk you to the door."

The stars were bright, and I felt a little dizzy as I looked up at them. My sweater slipped off my shoulder and Paul caught it, leaving his arm around me.

"Nice night," he said.

I tried to hold my shoulders very still.

On the porch, in the dim light, he didn't seem like Julia's brother. I turned to say thank-you, and my shifting weight made a board in the porch floor squeak.

For some reason, the sound made me giggle and Paul smile. Then he bent and kissed me quickly, his lips together, warm and dry on mine.

The next day, Paul asked me if I'd like to go to a matinee of *Cat People*.

"He asked you *out*?" Mary Ann squeaked on the phone. "On a *date*?"

"No! Just to an afternoon movie." I didn't tell her about the kiss, which he had probably meant just to be friendly.

The Iowa Theater wasn't crowded. When Paul and I entered from the bright spring sunshine, the feature was just starting.

"Wait," he whispered, taking my arm until our eyes adjusted. He smelled nice in a way I couldn't explain.

After the movie, we drove to the Cottage and got ice cream and took it out to the Chautauqua Park. We sat in the car and ate with little wooden spoons, Paul holding the carton.

Before he took me home, he tucked a strand of hair behind my ear and kissed me again. Our mouths were cold and sweet from the ice cream, but something deep inside me melted. Paul had probably kissed a lot of girls.

He picked me up after school every afternoon that first week. Dad and Mama never paid attention to how I was spending my time. Ages ago, they'd decided that I was responsible or that, if I wasn't, Jim would look after me. And if Jim noticed I stopped dropping by his office after school, he didn't say anything. Only Mary Ann knew.

"Why would a college boy, practically a relative, fall for a sixteen-year-old?" Mary Ann worried over our lunchtime tuna-salad sandwiches at Schoppes' Café.

I couldn't think of an answer except that maybe this was how it happened. This was the way a girl went from playing with dolls and looking through catalogues with friends to the next stage of life. It was a mystery. Mary Ann would understand when it happened to her.

"I don't know why," I told her, putting a nickel in the jukebox and playing Dick Jurgens's "Happy in Love."

❦

A couple of weeks later Dad, Mama, and I were invited to the Goodwins' for a Sunday evening dinner. Their house was the nicest in Jefferson, and the only one with a swimming pool, which sparkled at the back of a large yard glowing with bleeding hearts and tulips.

Mama wanted to walk through the gardens, so we ended up at the back door, and Paul let us in. As he greeted us, his eyes brushed my bare arms, tan from the sunbathing Mary Ann and I had done yesterday. I could tell by his manner that he felt the same way I did—sort of abashed that we were flying under false colors. But it was just all so *family* that it was kind of embarrassing to admit we were dating. We should have confessed to it. The longer we waited, the harder it got. And, truthfully, the secrecy was sort of fun.

The kitchen was fragrant with the rosemary that Mrs. Goodwin had put in with her pot roast. In the dining room, Julia and Jim were setting the huge mahogany table with bone china. And my brother Amos and his wife, Glenna, were in the living room, where their baby, Elizabeth, held the Goodwins captive with just a flick of her little bootied foot.

"Come and see your precious niece," Mrs. Goodwin called to me, shaking a silver rattle over Elizabeth and running her voice up in a trill that made the baby churn her fat legs.

The baby *was* sweet, looking kind of like an infant version of Mama, with dark eyes and a solemn expression. Mama returned the baby's sober gaze, and Dad held a finger down for Elizabeth to clasp.

"I do wish Julia and Jim would give us a grandchild," Mrs. Goodwin said to Mama. "You're so lucky."

Julia had stepped into the room just then with a question for her mother on her face, but when she heard Mrs. Goodwin's words, she turned silently and walked away. Mama and Dad and the Goodwins were so focused on the baby that they didn't notice, and I pretended I didn't either.

I held the baby for a minute to make Amos and Glenna happy, and then I handed her to Mrs. Goodwin, who was clearly just itching for her. Mrs. Goodwin babbled over Elizabeth while Mama's eyes ranged the sets of books on one wall.

As I went back through the dining room looking for Paul, Jim and Julia were taking goblets out of the china cupboard. Jim's way with Julia said he knew about her hurt. My brother liked to fix things for people he loved. It must have grieved him that he couldn't fix the world for her.

When we were seated around the table a while later, Mr. Goodwin raised his goblet of lemonade for a toast. "To our boy going off to fight in the war," he said, his voice hoarse. "May God bring him home safe."

"To Paul," we murmured, clinking our glasses.

Paul's face flushed at the attention, and I was so proud of him. Our eyes met. *Let's tell them.*

"Though we haven't seen much of him," Mr. Goodwin said, raising his eyebrows and sort of wiggling them.

"Then I'll bet it's a girl," Amos said, laughing.

People glanced at one another, then at Paul, with teasing implications that made it impossible to go ahead and say what we'd been going to say.

I woke up each morning staring at the calendar that hung on my bedroom wall. A Pears Soap girl gazed back at me, her face radiant. But I thought her eyes looked sadder each day, as if she knew that when I turned the calendar page, Paul would be gone. And some of the boys never came back. Max Donoho had been killed at Pearl Harbor. Luther McMillan in the Battle of the Coral Sea.

Paul had to be scared. Who wouldn't be?

Saturday morning, I sat on the front porch of the little house Mama and Dad rented on East Harrison. Along the edge of the porch, Dad had stacked cartons of vanilla and other kitchen spices that he sold door-to-door for Watkins. I rested the picnic basket on top of the cartons while I waited for Paul. The peanut butter cookies that I'd gotten up early to make were still a little warm, and their smell drifted out from the napkin they were wrapped in.

A rose climbed a trellis on the porch. The buds were barely starting to open, showing little furls of red at the tips. I broke off one and slid it through the eyelet collar on my blouse.

A car slowed and stopped, and I was halfway down the sidewalk before I realized it was Jim.

"Where are you off to?" he asked. "I take my eye off you for a minute and look what happens. You're awfully . . . grown-up these days."

Over his shoulder, I saw Paul's car. He parked behind Jim and got out, standing with the door open, waiting. I waved and smiled. "Hi!" I called.

Jim turned and raised his hand in greeting, too. He was smiling, but he looked a little puzzled as Paul came up the sidewalk. "What are you up to?" Jim asked.

Paul wasn't as tall as Jim. But his face still looked like I felt inside—like we were at the very edge of someplace wonderful. Jim's face was so serious these days, even when he smiled.

"Well, I came by for Cathy," Paul explained. "We thought we might drive out to Squirrel Hollow for a picnic."

Jim's eyebrows pulled together. Not in a frown exactly— more to understand Paul's meaning. "You're leaving soon," he said to Paul.

I don't think he meant it to sound unfriendly, but Paul blinked.

"Yep. Camp Dodge for a few days, and then on to Fort Benning, Georgia, and other army camps."

Two days. That's all we had. I turned and ran back to the porch for the picnic basket.

The boys shipping out of Camp Dodge for Fort Benning and other army camps got to say good-bye to their families at the train station that morning. We'd have about half an hour, Paul had written to his parents.

Because of gas rationing, we were all driving down together in the Goodwins' Lincoln—Mr. and Mrs. Goodwin, Jim and Julia, Amos and me. I had to hurry and get dressed—make myself pretty, so Paul wouldn't be able to forget me.

I sat down in front of the mirror and brushed my hair, which Paul said was the color of moonlight. The tiny bottle of Lucien Lelong perfume he'd given me sat on the vanity with my nail polishes and lipsticks that I'd bought at Potter's Drugstore with Mary Ann. Tailspin was the name of the fragrance.

Tailspin.

My hands started shaking, so I slid them between my silky slip and the vanity bench, sitting on them, shutting my eyes, counting to ten. He hadn't meant it to happen, that last night. But there'd been no stopping.

I took a deep breath and looked at myself in the mirror,

trying to see if it was written on my face. Would people know just by seeing us together?

The Pears Soap girl on the wall calendar watched me as I placed a dot of Paul's perfume between my breasts, just above the tiny rose appliqué on my white brassiere. The look in her eye was understanding as she tucked a blossom into her hair.

On the drive to Des Moines, Julia sat in the front between her parents, and I sat in the back between my brothers. Probably only Jim had even a tiny hint that I was going to say good-bye to the boy I was crazy in love with.

"You'll be making this trip to see *me* off before too long," he announced when we were somewhere between Jefferson and Perry.

Julia glanced back at him, her eyes flashing with instant tears, but there was no surprise on her face.

I think I gasped. "When?"

Mr. Goodwin looked at Jim in the rearview mirror. "Is that what the draft board says?"

"No. They say because I'm twenty-seven and married, probably not until early next year," Jim admitted.

Then he should wait. I knew my brother would have to go sometime, but not yet. I couldn't spare Paul and him both. And surely Julia felt the same way.

"You could wait even longer if you started a family," Mr. Goodwin said.

I sensed Julia's shoulders stiffen underneath her pale blue spring suit.

"Art—" Mrs. Goodwin started to say.

"I don't want to wait," Jim cut in. "Julia and I have decided. The sooner I go, the sooner I can come home."

I squeezed my hands, feeling like I might get carsick.

"So when are you going?" Amos demanded, staring out the window at the lines of spring-green corn shoots striping the fields. Some of the fields had the orange G&S signs posted at the end of the rows, with the number of the hybrid printed on them. Amos was five years older than Jim and had a deferment to keep working in farming, an essential industry. Plus, he was married with a child. He probably felt guilty.

"September," Jim said. Then he changed the subject, looking at me. "You'll be back in school then. A senior. Almost grown-up."

I nodded, staring out the window, trying not to cry, trying not to make things harder for Jim. But September was only three months away.

We got to the train station early and sat outside on benches in the June breeze, waiting for the army bus from Camp Dodge.

What would I say when I saw Paul? How would I act?

Big billowing clouds floated overhead, moving the Des Moines skyline in and out of shadow. A gull from the river cried overhead. Julia and her mother were so smart in their suits and hats and white gloves. I felt babyish in my saddle oxfords and bobby socks.

When the soldiers got off the bus, at first they all looked alike in their khaki uniforms. When I saw Paul, I made myself not wave, not run to him.

He hurried over and shook hands with his dad and Jim and Amos. He hugged his mom and sister. And then he was standing in front of me.

He held out his hands. "Cathy."

I stood up, making myself smile, feeling him tremble slightly.

"Well, we all made it, son," Mr. Goodwin said. "Can we buy you a cup of coffee and a sandwich before you go?"

"Sure."

But all the other families had the same idea. How do you spend your last thirty minutes with a person you love? Some of the girlfriends, wives, and mothers were crying, but mostly people were acting hearty, like they were suddenly consumed with hunger and thirst. The line in front of the canteen was long and unorganized.

"Just get me a cup of coffee, will ya?" Paul said quietly to Jim, and then he tugged on my hand and pulled me to the other side of a large, square pillar.

I really looked into his eyes for the first time today. We didn't touch except for our hands.

"I didn't mean it to happen," he said, so low only I could hear.

I nodded, barely able to swallow.

"But I'm not sorry," he said.

I shook my head.

We stood like that, just holding hands and looking at each other. He whispered, "I'll always take care of you, Cathy. You know that."

Then we eased back into line, talking about the drive down, whether the corn looked good. Jim handed Paul a cup of coffee and he walked over to join his parents by Gate 5, where he'd be boarding in just a few minutes.

Jim bought me a Coke and I sipped it, grateful to be holding the ice-cold glass. Paul glanced at me now and then with a smile that only the two of us understood.

Chapter Two

I HEARD MARY ANN on the front porch. "Hey, you ready?" she called softly through my open bedroom window.

"Almost," I said, going to the screen. The sun wasn't up yet, but the horizon showed a line of red. The sticky July air made me feel like I needed a bath already.

I listened to the low rumble from the west. "Is that thunder?"

"I imagine." She slapped at a mosquito. "It's like a jungle out here."

"Come in if you want to. I still have to fill my Thermos."

"I'll wait on the swing. It's cooler."

Mama and Dad were still in bed. Without turning on the kitchen light, I emptied an ice tray into my gallon Thermos and filled it to the brim with water. I put the sandwich I'd made the night before into a paper bag.

I had on a pair of overalls that Mary Ann's brother had outgrown, and a white sleeveless blouse. My sanitary napkin chafed between my legs. I hadn't started yet, but I surely would today, and the cornfield gave no privacy.

I grabbed the old hunting shirt of Dad's I wore to keep the corn leaves from shredding my arms.

"Ready," I told Mary Ann, dropping my stuff in the swing.

The paperboy was pedaling by on his bicycle, the chain squeaking. "Catch," he called, when he saw me. The folded square sailed toward me out of the darkness and I missed. When the newspaper hit my chest I cried out.

Mary Ann jumped up. "What?"

I felt a course of tears on my face. I shook my head.

"What happened?" she insisted.

"Oh, it just hurt," I said, trying to laugh it off, but starting to cry all over again, keeping my arms crossed over my chest, not wanting to move, knowing my nipples would ache at the slightest motion.

"Stupid paper boy," Mary Ann muttered. "Does it still hurt?"

I nodded. "Kind of." We needed to get going. The crew truck picked us up on the square at six. "I'll start my period today, then it will be better."

Mary Ann nodded, looking at me.

I felt a typhoon of tears coming, and I snatched my stuff and pulled Mary Ann along beside me. I didn't want Mama and Dad to hear. Halfway down the block, I collapsed on the other side of a big elm and leaned against it.

"It can't happen the first time," I told her, wiping my face on Dad's shirt. That's what girls said. So I hadn't worried when I'd missed my period last month.

"What can't happen the first time?" Mary Ann asked, staring at me.

"You know!" I started to sob again. "Oh God, Mary Ann. *You know!*"

She let me bury my face in her neck like she was my mother. She petted my hair. I hoped nobody was up early, looking out their front windows.

"The night before Paul left," I finally whispered. "It just happened. Nobody meant it to."

I felt her flinch. Mary Ann didn't even have a boyfriend.

Around the corner, in front of the courthouse, the crew truck sounded the horn for loading. We had only five minutes.

I pulled away. "Let's go," I said. "A hard day's work will fix things." But Mary Ann looked so wretched that I started to cry again.

We rode in the back of the truck out to the farm where we'd spend the day going along the rows and pulling the tassels off the corn plants. But the crew boss had us wait to see what the weather was going to do. For a while, thunder and lightning boomed and flashed. Then the rain came down so hard that we were soaked instantly. It felt good, like it was washing away everything from my body, cleansing me. Mary Ann and I looked at each other, our hair streaming water, knowing we could cry all we wanted and nobody would suspect. Crying invisibly in the rain made me happier—that and the warm, wet feeling between my legs.

Fairly quickly, the downpour tapered off, but a steady rain seemed to settle in to stay. About eight thirty, the truck took us back to town. Mary Ann came to my house. Dad had left for work and Mama was doing the breakfast dishes.

In my bedroom, we stripped off our wet clothes. My sanitary napkin was wet, but only with rain. As I passed Mary Ann panties and a bra from my drawer, I saw her glance at my nipples. I didn't try to hide their darkness anymore.

In our fresh underwear, we sat on my unmade bed and dried our hair. And then we took turns painting each other's toenails. As Mary Ann held my foot in her lap and brushed on polish, I gave myself over to the light tickle of the brush.

"You'll have to go see Dr. Stedman," she said matter-of-factly, setting aside my one foot and taking up the other one.

I nodded without opening my eyes. I had to write to Paul.

I took Paul's letter into my bedroom, closed the door, and sat down on the bed. Had he gotten my news before he wrote it?

My hands were shaking so hard I had to spread out the sheets of stationery against my legs so I could read what he had written.

Tuesday, July 30, 1942

Cathy, I got the letter.

The way he wrote "*the* letter" sounded cold. Did he mean to sound cold?

I feel a million miles away from you.

We're crammed in the barracks so tight I can hear the pulse of the guy in the next bunk. If I could just get off by myself for a while and think about things . . .

Think about things was all I ever did. I wished I could quit.

(Later) I'm trying to come to grips with your news. I guess I knew it <u>could</u> happen, but I didn't think it would.

If we could just start over. Undo this.

And the prospect of beginning a family right now seems terrifying. You're only sixteen.

And still in high school.

I'm only twenty.

But he was a guy and could walk away from this and nobody would ever know. I was trapped.

And who knows where I'll be in six months? The thing is, I'm just surprised.

I tried to brace myself.

(Later) I've never said I love you.

But I thought he did. I thought he just didn't have time to say it because everything happened so fast.

Maybe I wasn't even sure. But believe it or not, as I rode the train down here six weeks ago, getting farther away from you by the minute, I was thinking about how I'd like to ask you to marry me after the war.

Before I even told him about the baby?

I was thinking we'd be older then and everything would be settled.

But now this.

I want you to know two things—One: I love you. Two: I'll take care of you.

My tears blurred the ink, but I could still read the next sentence just fine.

And this means getting married now.

I let out a cry of joy and fell back on the bed, holding up the last page.

(Later, after chow) I think I have a plan worked out. I can't get home until the end of August when I'm done with officer training. But then I'll have a few days' leave. I'll come home, we'll tell the families, we'll get married.

I pressed the letter over my heart. How could I have doubted him?

> They'll get used to the idea fast enough. It's not like we'll
> be the first people in the history of the human race to
> have to do this.

Still. It would be awful. I could hardly bear to think of the look on Jim's face. And of Mama and Dad's reaction. And it would embarrass everybody so much. What people would say!

> But, Cathy, it will be hard for you around town. So I
> think that after we're married, you should follow me.
> Did I tell you I have a good shot at code school? If I
> make it, I'll be sent to a school somewhere in Virginia,
> which means I'll be stateside for another six months after
> OCS. And you could follow me to the base. Which means
> we might get this little Goodwin born before I have to
> leave, if I'm counting right.
> And after that, we'll just have to wing it. But you'll be a
> married woman with a baby by then, and I'll be an army
> intelligence officer. Doesn't sound too bad, does it?

I kissed the sheet of paper.

> Meanwhile, you said that Mary Ann is the only person
> who knows. Let's keep it that way until I get home. I don't
> want you to have to stand up to the family without me.
> Let's face it, this is going to be a big shock to them.

Amen.

I wish we were out at Spring Lake together right now. I wish we were anywhere together right now. I could write pages and pages about what I wish. But I'm going to stop and put this in the mail because I don't want you worrying any longer than you have to about how I took the news.

I put the letter back in the envelope and just sat on the edge of the bed staring at the Pears Soap girl who'd seen me go from a child to practically a married woman in only three months. I was so lucky Paul loved me and wanted to marry me.

In late August, Mary Ann and I were looking in the windows of the Susan Shop on the north side of the square. I was hungry enough to gnaw on the fake apple in the window, in front of the sign that read BACK TO SCHOOL.

"Mom says I can get two outfits," Mary Ann said. "I can't believe school's starting next week."

"I can't believe Paul will be home next week."

Mary Ann squeezed my arm. She was the only person who knew I wouldn't be returning to high school. Jim was planning to enlist soon, and I was glad I was going away so I wouldn't miss him so much.

Poor Julia. Jim leaving and her faced with the news that there was going to be a grandchild in the Goodwin family. Maybe I should tell Jim and Julia. But Paul had said to wait.

"Let's go in," Mary Ann said. "I want to try on that orange sweater."

A fan sat on the dressing-room floor, pointed upward. I stood in front of it for a minute, then unbuttoned my skirt before I sat down on the corner bench and let out a groan of ease as I rubbed the imprint left by my too-tight waistband.

I met Mary Ann's eyes in the mirror. "Soon," I said.

She knew I meant soon I wouldn't always have to be sucking in my stomach and wearing my loosest clothes because I'd be a respectable married woman off in Virginia where people didn't know Paul and I had just gotten married.

"That sweater looks nice on you," I told her.

Mary Ann turned, glancing over her shoulder into the mirror. "It doesn't make me look fat?" she asked. "You know, like a pumpkin?"

I laughed. "No. You look pretty. I'm the one who looks fat."

The Susan Shop carried maternity clothes, and I'd snuck a look at them as I came in. Short-sleeved dark tops, like little tents with white collars. Would Paul still think I was pretty when I started to really show?

I leaned my head against the wall, shutting my eyes, imagining how wonderful it would be to hold his hand, to feel his safe, solid warmth beside me. I tried sometimes to think of the words we'd use to tell the family. Nothing seemed to work when I thought about it, but Paul would know what to say.

I must have sighed or something, because Mary Ann said, "What?"

"Oh, I just want to get it over with," I said, opening my eyes. "Telling our families," I whispered.

Mary Ann nodded. "It'll be okay." But her eyes betrayed the truth. I'd go through life marked as a girl who had to get married. And our families would never live it down, no matter how politely people acted.

My stomach rumbled and I put my hand over it, saying, "Shh." We got the giggles then, but I thought about the baby growing inside me. I didn't feel anything yet, but Dr. Stedman said I would in another month or two. "You need to tell your family," he'd said, helping me off the table. When I explained the baby's father would be home from the army the first of September and we were getting married, he'd patted me on the shoulder and said, "Good, good. A baby needs a father." As I paid for the visit with my detasseling money, I wondered how many secrets Dr. Stedman and his kind nurse, Eunice, kept.

"So should I get this sweater?" Mary Ann asked, pulling it off and putting her sleeveless linen blouse back on.

"Yes," I said, "then let's have lunch. I'm starving."

Mary Ann rolled her eyes. I was always starving.

Schoppes' was loud and bustling. We took seats at the counter, turning to face each other so our knees touched, talking while we waited for our food.

"I'll really miss you," she said quietly. "Who'd ever have thought I'd do senior year by myself?"

"You'll find a new friend." I felt tears coming. "You're a good person, Mary Ann." I bit my lip, not wanting to cry in public.

We turned back to the counter, sipping our Cokes. The icy sting steadied me, and I was able to take a deep breath and keep my voice even. "I don't know how I would have survived this without you."

She shrugged, drawing on her straw, keeping her eyes lowered, but I saw the gleam of tears between her lashes.

After lunch, Mary Ann wanted to do a little more shopping, but my back hurt and I felt exhausted, so I headed home, scurrying from one patch of shade to the next.

When I walked by Mr. Goodwin's real estate and insurance office, I saw Jim's car parked in front and I took it as a sign of some kind. My whole life, Jim had looked after me. He said he'd changed my diapers when I was a baby. And now that I was going to have a baby, I should tell him myself rather than let him hear the news from Paul.

I got in the car and waited. Jim had left the windows down, and a breeze cooled the sweat on my face and arms. Yesterday's newspaper lay on the seat, and I picked it up and fanned myself. I watched the door to the office, trying to think of how I'd tell Jim. I decided to just blurt it out with whatever words came to me.

I leaned back in the seat, relaxing for the first time in what seemed like ages, now that everything was set in motion. I'd tell Jim the minute he got in the car, marry Paul next week, and live happily ever after. I shut my eyes, thinking about the sweet little baby layettes I'd seen in the Sears Roebuck catalogue. Paul and I could look at them together when he got home, and I'd let him choose the one he liked best. A fly kept pestering me, landing first on my arm, then my neck, then my cheek. But even so, I still fell asleep in the heat of the car.

I woke up when Jim opened his door.

"Hi," I said, sitting up straight, the back of my blouse wet. My mouth was dry and my head hurt a little. But I went ahead with my resolve. "Jim, I've got to tell you—"

And then I saw how pale he was. Freckles I hadn't seen in years were marked on his face like somebody had pounded them there with crayons. His mouth had thinned out in a harsh line. He'd gotten *old*.

"What is it?"

Had something happened to Mama or Dad? Or Amos? Or Julia?

He looked at me, his eyes not quite focused. "Paul," he said.

What about Paul?

And then I knew. Somehow Jim had found out. Maybe Paul had written to his dad to prepare him, and Mr. Goodwin had told Jim.

"But we're getting married," I exclaimed. "I'm sorry, Jim, and so's Paul. We should have waited, but we didn't mean it to happen. And he's doing the right thing. That's what I'd come to tell you. About"—instinctively my hands went over my stomach—"about the baby."

Jim's eyes came into full focus on me. "What?" The word came out like all the breath left in him.

"The baby. I'm having a baby. Paul and I are getting married." It sounded so easy and sensible and clear once I said it aloud to Jim. Why had I waited so long?

Jim looked at me for a minute and then he took my hand, squeezing it hard. "My poor Cathy," he said.

Chapter Three

JIM SAID THERE had been a jeep accident on the base. The driver had been badly hurt. Paul had been killed. Jim took me home and stayed with me as long as he could, but he had to meet Julia and her mother, who were coming home from Des Moines on the three thirty train. I hid in my bedroom, curled up on the bed with my knees almost to my chin, my skirt unbuttoned.

Jim's quiet voice talking to Mama was punctuated by her exclamation, and I knew he'd told her. After he left, she slipped in, put her hand to my forehead, and smoothed back my hair. Then she went away.

Sunlight crept through the west window, across my dressing table, and the little crystal vial of perfume that Paul had given me scattered the light like a prism. I stared at the moon of my bare knee and willed it to move half an inch, but it wouldn't.

Amos came and talked to Mama. At first their voices were loud and shocked over the terrible accident, then furtive, with long silences. The tears burned my face. Mama was telling Amos.

After a while, Amos went away and the telephone began to ring. I listened to Mama's conversations, saying yes, Paul had been killed in an accident on the base, right before he finished his officer's training. His family had been expecting him home next week. Wasn't it terrible?

Dad came up on the porch, and the screen door banged behind him. Mrs. Kennedy, a customer on his Watkins route, had heard the news and told him. Mama drew him toward the back of the house with her conversation, and I heard their voices drop to talk about the other thing. Now Dad knew, too.

Eventually the sun went down, the light growing paler and paler in my bedroom. I listened to house sounds, people coming and going, talking. I needed to pee so badly I thought I'd burst, but I couldn't move. And if I went outside of my room, people would see me, and I couldn't stand that. I would turn to ash if anyone who knew looked at me.

I stared at the last of the pale twilight, silhouetting a pillar of the porch railing and the climbing rose. My hearing became exceptional. I heard Mama and Dad putting down the salt and pepper shakers on the kitchen table. I heard a bird in the linden tree settling her feathers for the night.

I heard Mary Ann's footsteps even before she came up on the porch.

"I need to turn a light on," she said, coming into my room. Without waiting for an answer, she groped her way to my desk and flicked on my reading lamp. I put my hands over my face.

"I didn't hear until just a few minutes ago because we went out to my grandma's this afternoon and stayed for supper," Mary Ann said, coming to sit on the bed beside me. Her voice had a thick, plugged-up sound.

We occupied my bed in silence until the phone rang again.

"It's Jim," Mama said, coming to my door. "He wants to talk to you."

Why couldn't he come here and talk to me?

Mary Ann stood up, taking my hands, helping me off the bed. The phone was in the hall. Mama's back disappeared into the kitchen as I came out of my room, and I was glad.

Jim kept his voice very low. "Cathy, I'm at the Goodwins'. I've told Julia and her parents."

A squeak of pain escaped me. Soon everybody would know. I cupped my hands over the receiver and made myself ask the question. "Are they mad?"

Jim sighed. "They've got so much to deal with right now."

A tear ran across my cheek and settled where the receiver was pressed to my face. My hands smelled salty.

"We'll work things out somehow," he said. "In a few days. Try not to worry." His voice sounded thin. "I'll fix it."

On Saturday, they had Paul's funeral. Mama said I should stay home, that she'd say I had a bad summer cold. Dad wore his best suit and looked tall and distinguished with his silver hair. When his eyes met mine, his expression wasn't cold, exactly; it was just bewildered. And hurt. I hugged my shoulders and looked away.

On Monday, Jim and Amos and I went to Chicago in Amos's big Buick. I sat in the front seat between my brothers, my suitcase in the back. Dr. Stedman had given them the name of a home in Chicago for girls in my predicament, and Amos said the timing was critical. We wanted people to think I was going away to boarding school.

Hills of corn rolled away to the horizon on both sides of the road.

"Paul and I were getting married tomorrow," I said. "We were." I wanted them to acknowledge that Paul had really loved me. And everything would have been all right if he hadn't gotten killed.

I saw Amos checking the corn rows for G&S signs. "The oldest story in the book," he muttered. "You're not old enough to get married anyway." I felt Jim look at Amos, but Amos went on. "The Goodwins don't need this scandal on top of everything else. And it's killing Mama and Dad."

"Shut up, Amos," Jim said. "Just *shut up*."

I cried, watching blurs of corn go by.

"Cathy, we don't want your life ruined," Jim explained after a while, his voice sounding disconnected, as if he were thinking about something else. "Eventually, things will go back to being the way they were."

Without Paul, how could things ever go back to being the way they were?

He and Amos had their windows open, and my hair blew into my face. I tried to hold it back for a while, then I quit. What difference did looking pretty make anymore?

I thought of Margaret Lane, an unmarried woman who lived in one of the cabins out at the Kozy Court. She had a little girl I saw around town. The child—who had beautiful platinum-colored hair—was always shabby and alone. People said Margaret put food on the table by "entertaining" men who stayed at the travel court, and they said the child was illegitimate. A bastard. I didn't want to end up like Margaret, with too much lipstick and a hunted look.

Amos glanced at his gold Bulova watch. "We should be there by two."

I shut my eyes, looking at my old dreams. They were fading like photographs left in the sunlight, but I could still see myself in a little hat with a feather held on by a rhinestone pin. I was wearing a suit like a grown woman, a silk blouse with a lace collar, and a corsage of roses. Paul, smiling just enough to show the tiny space between his strong, white teeth, looked handsome in his military uniform. We'd gotten married down at the courthouse and had stopped by Nielsen's Photography on the way home to have our wedding portrait made.

And there we were later, riding the long train to Virginia. Paul had his arm around me, his billed army cap tilted back, and he was grinning. I was looking up at him. Mr. and Mrs. Paul Goodwin.

And much later, we were in a tiny apartment somewhere. I was standing at the stove stirring a pot of soup. My tentlike maternity top billowed out in front, and Paul was kissing my neck.

Back in the real world, between Iowa City and the river, we met a nearly endless army convoy going west. The canvas sides of the trucks rattled and snapped in the wind. I began to count the trucks to keep from thinking.

The sun was hot and the road stank of exhaust.

After we'd gone about a mile without meeting any more, I said, "Thirty-seven."

"What?" Jim asked.

"Thirty-seven. Army trucks."

He nodded, staring out the window.

Would he still enlist this month like he'd planned? If something happened to Jim, too, I'd die.

A low iron fence surrounded the home for unwed mothers. It looked more like a prison than the slightly run-down mansion it was. There was a grocery store and a Salvation Army depot across the street. The next block down were brownstones, and beyond that I thought I saw a movie marquee.

We had an appointment. The Snow family. I felt my face blazing as an office girl led us into a room that had probably once been a gracious side porch. I felt as naked as if I had left my clothes at home. Jim's face was red, too, but I was grateful that Amos looked as if he might have come to see about buying the Persian rug on the floor.

A woman introduced herself to us as a social worker, extending her hand to Amos, then Jim, then me. Although it was hot in the room, her hand was dry and cool.

We all sat down, and she said, "Tell me how things are." She looked at me.

I looked at Jim, and he and Amos began to explain the whole humiliating story. When they were finished, the social worker talked about the philosophy of the home. I tried to focus on birds singing from bushes that pressed against the screened windows as she explained that the goal of the home was to allow young women to go through their pregnancies in privacy and then return to their communities with as little disruption to their lives as possible.

I heard a burst of voices and then silence as somebody opened and slammed a door nearby. After their babies were born, the social worker explained, the girls would go home to normal lives, and hopefully eventually marry and have other children.

The ceiling creaked from footsteps overhead. The babies, of course, she went on, were placed for adoption with couples who could provide wholesome, stable homes.

The smell of simmering tomatoes drifted through the open windows, and a line of sweat popped out on my forehead. The girls didn't see their babies, the social worker told us. After they were delivered, the infants were taken immediately to the hospital's nursery and turned over to their new families as soon as the doctor pronounced them healthy and ready. The girls could return to the home until they were strong enough to leave—usually a week or two after the baby was born.

I crossed my legs, desperate to go to the bathroom. Everything was completely confidential, the social worker went on. Any record that I had ever been here would be permanently sealed, as would the adoption records. I would never know who my baby had been placed with, and my baby would never know who its mother was. It was all for the best, she said. I would be "rehabilitated to society" and my baby would have a good home, free from any stigma of illegitimacy.

Margaret Lane and her beautiful little silver-haired girl flashed through my mind again.

"What are you telling people in your hometown about why Cathy has disappeared from daily life?" the social worker asked.

"That she's going to boarding school," Amos said. "Here in Chicago. And next year, she really will go to boarding school..."

Boarding school? Dad sold Watkins products to farmers—double-strength imitation vanilla, cooking spices, liniment, fly spray for horses, mineral supplements for hogs. We couldn't even afford to own a house.

Amos continued. "... except people at home will think she's away at college."

The social worker said, "That's a good solution for families who can afford it."

Amos nodded. "I can."

"Where's the bathroom?" I asked, desperate to get away.

It was snowing lightly, the wind blowing the flakes almost horizontally, the midday as gray as dawn.

"Company for you, Cathy," Nella said, poking her head in the sunroom, which, according to one of the girls, may as well have been called the dim room.

The handful of other girls were listening to the radio or reading or doing the counted cross-stitch that one of the volunteers had taught us. They glanced at me with envy.

Jim had said in his last letter that he and Julia would take the train into Chicago this weekend. But in the visiting room, only Julia waited on the divan, her purse in her lap.

"Jim couldn't come," she said quickly. "He's sick. But he didn't want you to be disappointed."

I couldn't keep the regret from showing on my face. I wanted to see my brother so much. "What's wrong?" I asked.

"A chest cold. He's been running a fever and hasn't been able to go to work for a couple of days. Dr. Stedman came by the house yesterday and said Jim shouldn't travel."

The bad news made me sink into a chair. I rested my hand on my belly, then yanked it off because the people at the home said we shouldn't get attached. The girls who stroked their bellies got bad looks from the nurses and social workers. *Don't worry about what's happening down there*, one of the nurses was always telling us. *We'll take care of all that, and soon you'll be good as new.* We may as well have been magicians' assistants who'd gotten inside the box and been successfully sawed in half, leaving public space between the two parts of our bodies.

"I hope Jim's okay," I said.

Julia nodded, but she looked worried and worn out. "He just has a lot on his mind." Drops of moisture from the sleety snow were caught in her hair. She seemed thinner and older, and she probably resented being packed off to see me.

She ran her fingers over the wooden armrest of the divan, which was carved in the shape of a big cat's claw. The hides of animals, some silvery gray, some gold and black flecked, hung in the long narrow room where we took our meals. *Do you suppose we're eating that?* one of the girls had said last night, pointing to the gray thing. *Wolf stew*, somebody had giggled, and we all poked at our plates with new interest.

"How was the train trip?" I asked, wondering how long we'd be able to make polite conversation.

"Awful. Soldiers were sleeping in the aisles and under the seats. One got up and gave me his place."

Had he made her think of Paul?

"Your mother sent you some things," Julia said, opening a small train case.

Mama had written me a few letters, not referring to anything *down there*, as the nurses called it, but the letters had seemed to smell of home, and I'd slept with them on my pillow.

Julia handed me a hefty book. "This will make the time go fast."

Gone With the Wind. Mary Ann and I had seen the movie when we were thirteen and had not been able to talk of anything else for days. Scarlett knew about war and love and babies.

Mama also sent me a pair of knitted socks, not quite the same size, a pretty tin of Watkins lady's bath powder, and a calendar for next year, 1943.

I flipped through the pages, looking at the March picture of a field of crocuses. That's when the baby would arrive. As if called, the baby stirred and I gasped, dropping the calendar.

"What?" Julia cried, half rising from the divan.

I gripped the chair arms, determined not to touch my stomach, but shifting, making my own little movement, returning the greeting. "The baby moved," I whispered, wishing somebody would explain the mystery of what was happening to me.

Julia whitened and looked at my stomach. The color rushed back into her face in a bloom of embarrassment.

Didn't she ever think about how part of her brother

was still living? "We could have been double sisters-in-law," I said.

Julia's expression flickered, and then her cheeks glistened with tears. "I know."

"What do your parents . . . ?" I didn't know how to finish the question. What did they think of me? What did they think about the baby? They wanted a grandchild so desperately.

Julia put her hand over her mouth, starting to cry. "They're so sad," I think she said through her sobs. "Just so sad."

I handed her the fresh handkerchief from my smock pocket. We were all so sad, but maybe parents were special.

Finally, she blew her nose. "I'm sorry, Cathy," she said, squeezing her hands together and taking a deep breath, trying to quit crying, hiccupping. She raised her tear-filled eyes, intense with something, and they bore into mine.

A bubble of fear rose in me. "Is it Jim? Is he sicker than you said?"

She coughed with a half laugh and half sob and mopped her face. She shook her head. "I'm just so jealous of you. May God forgive me, I'm just so jealous of you."

And then I was bawling, too, and we were beside each other on the divan, hugging. "I'm sorry," I said, "sorry for everything." I felt her nod, her wet cheek against mine.

Finally, we started to breathe more or less normally, and she gave me her own handkerchief to use.

Julia took a deep breath. "Amos sends his best," she said. "He says to tell you he's on the trail of some good boarding schools."

She went ahead to talk about one in Chicago and one in Minnesota. I tried to seem interested, but I ached for my old high school, with the smell of varnish on the woodwork, for Mary Ann, for the after-school visits to Jim's office, for my old life.

We worked it out so Mary Ann could come to see me in late February, riding the train with Amos, who was meeting with a banker. The evening before, I asked my roommate, Janet, who was a beautician, to cut my hair. And after, because I couldn't reach my feet to do it myself, she also polished my toenails.

"You must have a hot date," she said, her dark humor making us laugh.

The next day, I watched out the window for Mary Ann and flung open the door as she came up the steps in her familiar gray coat with the velvet collar. We tried to throw our arms around each other's necks like we used to, but my belly got in the way.

"Oh," she said, stepping back.

I knew I looked fat, my face puffy and perspiring despite the cold. I'd put on a new maternity top Julia had sent me—white and deeply pleated, with roses embroidered around the collar, and my nail polish was rose-colored, too.

I led Mary Ann into the visiting room. The matron had said we could have lunch on trays together and spend all the time in there until Amos came to pick Mary Ann up after his meeting.

"Do you like my haircut?" I asked.

"It looks beautiful. Your hair *is* beautiful. It looks so thick. Is it thicker?"

"It happens sometimes when you're pregnant," I said. "You get hairier all over. Facial hair." The girls teased each other about our mustaches.

I saw her looking at my upper lip. "My hair's so light it doesn't show," I said. "But some of the girls—"

"Did I tell you Donald and I went to Spring Lake the other night? We've been going most weekends. They had the best orchestra."

She'd told me in her letters about dating Donald Williams, and I was glad Mary Ann had a boyfriend now. But we'd meant to have our boyfriends together, like we'd done everything else.

We sat silently for a few seconds and then both started to say something at once. She giggled and then went on talking about a history project that she and Nancy were working on.

"Do you see a lot of Nancy?" I asked, hoping the pinch of jealousy didn't show.

She shrugged. "Well, she's not you."

I tried to concentrate on the news about school, but excited voices drifted through the door. Olivia had been having contractions at breakfast. The nurse had examined her and said it might be the real thing, though she wasn't due for another week.

When one of the girls went to the hospital, those of us whose time was close followed her out the door with our eyes, knowing she was going where we would all eventually go.

"There's nothing to be afraid of," Miss Cramer, the nurse I liked best, always said. "Nature will get you through."

Afterward, the girls returned looking pale and emptied out. They weren't supposed to talk about giving birth. "Just put it all behind you," the social workers said. "It's best that way."

I heard the front door open. Mary Ann was in midsentence. "I need to see about something," I said, laying my hand on her arm.

In the foyer, Miss Cramer was helping Olivia on with her coat. Olivia's mouth made a line of pain, and her eyes glittered as Miss Cramer finished doing the last button. The stained-glass windows threw a glow over the two of them.

"Good luck," we all told her.

She tried to smile, then bit her lip and clutched her belly, her feet apart. Margaret, who was only sixteen and due next month, like me, started to cry.

"Now never mind," Miss Cramer said. "Olivia will be a trouper. The doctor will look after her."

Back in the visiting room, Mary Ann seemed almost foreign. "One of the girls is going to the hospital to deliver," I told her.

She nodded, her expression wavering between embarrassment and curiosity.

"Her name's Olivia," I said, sitting down, trying to get back into the spirit of a good gab, but the old world was starting to seem so far away. My mind kept going to Olivia.

"What do people back home think has happened to me?" I asked.

I read several expressions on Mary Ann's face before she finally said, "They're not sure."

I waited.

"Well, at first some people wondered. . . ." She gestured with her hands toward my bulging stomach. "But they don't have any basis for thinking that, because so far as anybody knew, you didn't have a boyfriend." She sighed. "So probably they don't think about it much at all, and just accept the idea that your family is doing so well that you've gone off to boarding school." After a minute, she added, "I guess they've just kind of forgotten about it."

They'd forgotten about me was what she meant. Like the earth closing after an earthquake, the landscape was just different.

Chapter Four

IN THE MORNING, I'd had two contractions so deep I thought my back might break. Miss Cramer examined me and said the process was beginning, but that it would probably be a few days. Maybe even a week.

I sat up on the examining table and she slid my shoes back on.

"How will—" I began. I wanted to know how my body would deliver me of such a vast weight? Were they sure I wouldn't just tear apart when it did? And the little baby growing inside me, how would it fare?

But I shook my head, feeling tears coming, and didn't try to finish the questions. Miss Cramer squeezed my hands and helped me off the table.

They tried to distract me with Monopoly in the sunroom. I would be the next of the girls to go, so I was everybody's pet.

"Sit here," Janet said, pointing to a chair by a window slightly open to let in the March springtime. The smell of the air made me homesick, and a patch of sun bounced off Boardwalk into my eyes.

"Let somebody take my place," I said after a few turns. I'd just landed on Chance.

"But you're winning," one of the girls said.

I shook my head.

"Want a foot rub?" Janet asked.

I heard the postman's ring. "Give my real estate and money to the bank. I'll bring in the mail."

Among the letters was one from Jim, who wrote me at least twice a week. I sat down in the ornate, straight-backed chair in the foyer and opened it.

> Cathy,
>
> Are the birds singing there? Julia and I took a walk on Sunday. We went clear out to the park and walked by the house where you and I and Amos were born. Do you remember it very well? And we walked by Noah's family's house. The gold star in the window made me want to bawl. Noah should have come home. Who would have guessed when we were boys that he'd even go to a place called North Africa, much less die there when he was twenty-seven years old?
>
> You need to know that I got my letter from the draft board last Saturday. It's okay. I want to get it over with.

He was like me, probably, so afraid of what lay ahead that he could barely breathe.

> Julia and I hope to get a train into Chicago before I report, but things seem to be happening so fast now. Yet it's like they're in slow motion, too. It's strange.
>
> In case we don't get a chance to talk, I want you to trust Amos to help you. You have to forgive him for his protective attitude about Mama and Dad. Please remember, Cathy, that Mama and Dad were different when Amos was young. And different from that when I was young. None of us can help what time and life do to us.

Had he been thinking about me when he wrote that last sentence? Or did he think I could have helped it?

> The couple in Chicago that Amos has arranged for you to stay with afterward will be kind. I'm sure of it. He's known them for years, and they won't judge. Then you'll come home for the summer and you can count on Julia to be a friend. And Mary Ann. Around everybody else, just act like a newly rich kid home from her first year at boarding school. And next year, you really will be at one and you can start over. I know maybe you can't put this behind you, but I want you to try.
>
> It's hard for me to write this, but you need to be prepared for how the Goodwins feel. (Not Julia, of course.) But Paul's parents seem to think that if their

son had been involved with you, that they'd have known about it.

What! They didn't believe the baby was Paul's?

Try to forgive them. People kind of go crazy when they're grieving. And they're so determined that his memory not be tarnished.

My hands shook, imagining how they felt about me. It wasn't the least bit fair.

If Paul had lived, everything would have been so different. Mr. and Mrs. Goodwin would have been proud grandparents and I would have had a dozen beautiful layettes to wrap the baby in. Paul and I would have argued about what to name the baby and bought war bonds for her.

At the home, they told us not to wonder about the sex of the infant—that not getting involved in all that would make it easier to move on. But in my dreams I saw a blue-eyed girl with golden hair like Paul's and petite like me.

The baby kicked, rustling Jim's letter. Committing the forbidden, I put my hand on what I was pretty sure was her head. *Don't worry, Mary Suzanne.*

I finished Jim's letter and then gathered up the other mail and took it into the sunroom.

I couldn't go home without Jim. The sense of emptiness at the thought of his not being there was sharper than the taut fullness I felt as the baby quieted. Maybe the couple I'd be going to stay with after delivery would let me stay over the summer, too.

A few days later Miss Cramer settled me onto the chaise lounge at the little room at the end of the hallway. I knew what this meant. This was the room where we waited before we were taken to the hospital.

She slipped off my shoes and covered my feet and legs with a shawl. "Tucked or untucked?" she asked.

Her kindness and the joy of the pain sliding away sent tears down my cheeks. "Tucked," I whispered.

As she bent over to snug the shawl under my feet, her breasts in her starched white uniform looked so motherly. I knew she had a daughter about my age, and I wondered if she ever thanked God that her child hadn't ended up in a home for unwed mothers.

After she left to get me some water, I looked over what had probably once been a formal garden in the back. A line of old terracing shadowed the damp spring ground. Farther back, a pink bedspread hung airing from a clothesline.

Although she wasn't supposed to, when she'd returned from the hospital, Olivia had whispered to a couple of us what to expect. *It hurts like bejesus,* she'd said. *Like burning coals are being ripped out of you. It's unbelievably humiliating the way they spread you apart and strap you in. But you don't care about anything else, not a single thing, except getting it over with. Thank the good Lord they put up a white screen over your middle so you can't tell what's going on down there.*

We wanted to know if she'd seen the baby, but she said the minute the baby came out, they whisked it away. *Then they put us in rooms by ourselves, so we're not around the other babies coming for nursing.*

The pain started after me again, squeezing tighter and tighter and tighter. If it got hold of me, I would disappear into the whirlpool and nobody would ever see me again. I wanted Jim, Paul, Mama—anybody—to hold on to.

I tried to scream, but it came out as a gasp. "Miss Cramer!"

My sheets were wet with sweat, and Miss Cramer kept wiping my face with a cool cloth and spooning bits of ice into my mouth. The fires of pain would burn me up. What was happening to the baby? Why had she gone so still?

"Open the window," I begged between clenched teeth. "Mary Suzanne is getting too hot." Then I tried to get my hand over my mouth because I had spoken her name.

Miss Cramer caught my hand, and held it against my breasts. "Shh," she said. "She's fine. Everybody's fine."

Then the ceiling lights were rushing over me and I knew I was being moved.

In the room, white and bright, a nurse with a mask over her face slid a lamp toward me. "The spring weather is bringing on the babies," she said. "We're overflowing. Not an empty bed on the ward."

Miss Cramer's voice sounded different when she answered, and I glanced up to see her brown eyes looking at me from over the top of a mask, too.

When the big white screen, like Olivia had described, blocked out everything else, I knew it was about over.

I kept my eyes shut, trying to hide. I felt like I'd been sliced and cooked *down there*. The doctors and nurses said things to one another, and I may have heard the baby cry, but I'm not sure.

I finally turned loose of Miss Cramer's hand. She pulled sweaty strands of hair off my forehead then wiped my face. "Right as rain," she murmured, "right as rain."

I imagined summer drizzle rinsing away everything and thought of Mary Ann and the day we'd gone to detassel corn and I'd told her I was expecting.

"I'm going to leave you for a little bit," Miss Cramer said. "Go to the bathroom and get a bite to eat."

How many hours had she been with me, letting me clutch her hand as I yelled?

"Do you know it's nine thirty at night? It's almost past your bedtime," she joked. The breathy patter of her voice said she was worn-out, too. "They'll clean you up a little and roll you to your room. I'll be back in two shakes," she said, patting me.

A little while later, an attendant covered me with a clean blanket and rolled me out of the delivery room.

"The doctor sent the mother in 24B home," I heard someone say. "Put her in there—it's our only open bed."

I was trembling and weak when they helped me into a regular bed. The starched and ironed sheets made sliding sounds.

"How y'all, hon?" a voice on the other side of the curtain said. "Open that curtain," she demanded of the attendant folding the bleachy-smelling blanket over me.

The curtain swished back to show a woman with red hair and bright lipstick. "I cain't sleep and I'm dyin' of boredom." She said the word without the *r*, so it came out bo'edom. "I'm from Georgia. Y'all from around here?"

The attendant cranked up the head of my bed. They'd left me feeling so open, like my heart could slide away. How would I close up?

"Y'all from around here?" the woman asked again.

What could I say? *I've been staying in a home for unwed mothers?*

"My husband's in the service," I said.

She looked approving, nodding for more information. So I went on with my grand lie. What difference did it make now anyway?

"When I'm able to leave the hospital, we're moving to Virginia. He's going to code school there." And then I began to bawl. I cried until the stiff white pillowcase turned damp and limp. Soon they'd be bringing the papers for me to sign.

"Here they come," said the woman from Georgia, whose name turned out to be Madelyn. She glanced at her gold watch. "Right on schedule."

"Who?" I asked. Was she signing papers, too?

"The hun-n-ngry babies wanting their ten o'clock feeding, who else?" she said, beginning to unbutton her bed jacket.

A nurse lifted a blue wrapped bundle from a cartful of babies and sped across the room. "We're full up and short-handed," she said to Madelyn. "Can you manage by yourself?"

"After five of them, I wouldn't be surprised, hon." Madelyn took her baby.

The tiny red thing reminded me of a kitten with its eyes still shut. I wanted to look away, but couldn't.

"And here you go," the nurse said, handing a pink swaddled bundle into my arms. "Can you manage, too?"

My arms opened automatically to receive my baby, but my lips wouldn't move. She was about the size of a loaf of Wonder Bread and smelled warm and a little yeasty.

"Do you need help?" the nurse asked, half poised to turn back to the cart of babies.

Some were crying, but mine—Mary Suzanne—just turned her face toward my breasts. What harm would one time do? Miss Cramer could straighten it all out when she turned up.

"I'll help Cathy if she needs it," Madelyn said. "Go on. Shoo. Sounds like you got somebody starvin' in there."

The fearsome wonder of what I was going to do made my hand shake as I opened the front of my gown. It was like the one time Paul and I made love. There was no stopping now.

After, Mary Suzanne lay in the crook of my arm. I unwrapped her. I'd never get another chance to see her protruding belly, bandaged where a little thimble of a navel would someday be. I eased apart the tiny crevices of her elbows, knees, and thighs. I took off her pink booties and touched each toe. I caressed the knuckles of each finger and traced the curve of her ears and eyebrows.

"She's perfect, isn't she?" my roommate asked.

I nodded.

Miss Cramer would kill me. I should have told the nurse I wasn't supposed to see my baby, that she was being adopted.

I wrapped her back up, a gift to somebody. I would never know who. I whispered in her ear, "I love you, Mary Suzanne, and your daddy would have loved you, too."

Voices outside the door said I was about to be found out. I tucked her between my left arm and side where she could feel my heartbeat for a few seconds longer.

Jim and Julia came in, their movements quiet, their faces showing that they didn't belong on a maternity ward at this time of night.

"Shh," Jim said, smiling and putting a finger over his mouth. "The head nurse said we could step in for just a minute." He pulled the curtain shut between my bed and Madelyn's, keeping his gaze away from her.

"Jim! Oh, Jim." I reached my right arm out to him.

"How are you?" he asked, kissing my forehead, looking at my face, taking my hand.

"Okay." I curled my fingers around his.

He didn't notice the bundle in the shelter of the blanket. He stepped back and Julia took my other hand, squeezing it. I saw the skip in her eyes when she registered the baby.

"How long have you been here?" I asked.

"We got into Union Station about noon. We went by the house," he said, mindful of listening ears, "and then came here. We have to go back on the midnight train, which is why the nurse let us in for a minute."

The baby stirred in her swaddling. She might begin to cry. And Julia was looking at me. I had to explain.

"Jim, there's been a terrible mistake." I meant to tell him about the mistake of the crowded hospital and of me being put in a room with another nursing mother and the mix-up about bringing my baby to me. "A really terrible mistake."

I lifted Mary Suzanne so she lay on her stomach over my breasts. Her weight felt so good there I nearly passed out.

"My God!" Jim muttered, his voice low.

"Jim," I whispered, shutting my eyes and circling my hand on the baby's back. Her breath was brushing my neck with regular strokes.

After a time, I felt a hand on top of mine. It was Julia. Her face was clawed by emotion as she looked at the baby.

"Her name is Mary Suzanne," I confessed.

Julia's eyes shifted to mine. She nodded, tears bathing her face.

"Would you like to hold her?"

Julia glanced at Jim, whose face looked as if the ball of the world had begun unraveling into random bits of string.

Something flickered between them and Julia nodded, the corners of her mouth trembling between grief and joy. I lifted the baby into her arms.

The warm spot where Mary Suzanne had lain felt cool and a little damp. I pulled the covers over me.

"Oh, Jim, look," Julia said.

She rocked the baby with her whole body and bent down to show Mary Suzanne's face to Jim.

The baby's pink blanket against Julia's dark green suit made me think of the big hibiscus flowers in the sunroom at the home. A strand of Julia's hair slipped from the tortoiseshell comb that held it back and fell forward near the baby's face—a perfect match.

I thought of the little ragged illegitimate girl back home, marked forever. I couldn't do that. But Mary Suzanne was ours—mine and Julia's, in a way.

"Please?" I asked them.

Jill
1969

Chapter One

THE AUGUST MOON played on the ripples of Spring Lake.

"Mellow," Andy said, taking a hit and passing it to me. "Ray sure grows good shit."

"Yeah." I inhaled, savoring my high. God was in His heaven, and all was light with the world. No need to thank me for improving your poetry, Mr. Browning.

By the fire, Megan raised a stick with a tiny torch of a marshmallow flaming at the tip. Crissy and her boyfriend whispered to each other. I leaned against Andy's side and stared at the water. Moonlight touching the waves had woven little nets of silver—probably to catch the falling stars.

Whoa. The idea made me giggle as I rubbed my cheek against the softness of Andy's T-shirt. As he began to kiss me, the darkness and the sounds of the water and the popping of the beach fire wrapped us in privacy. We stretched out on the blanket and I curled my legs through his as his fingers, cool from our swim, stroked my belly.

The crack of tires on crushed rock startled me. There was always the chance that the sheriff's deputies would swoop in to ruin our fun. But the thump of Led Zeppelin's music signaled there were no deputies this time.

"Just Ray," Andy murmured, kissing my neck.

I propped myself up on an elbow as the headlights swept over us. Ray killed the lights but left his speakers cranked. Against the stars, I could see the roofline of the old Spring Lake dance hall, closed now. Ray and a girl in a long skirt and peasant blouse walked toward us, holding hands. The girl's jewelry made a musical tinkling sound.

"Rural Free Delivery," Ray said, tossing a packet of something toward us. It spun in the moonlight and then fell onto our blanket with a rattle.

Andy's fingers got tangled up with mine feeling for it. "Pretzels!" I announced.

"I want some!" Crissy called.

Ray stepped up to the fire, his arm around the girl. I didn't know her, but I could tell in the firelight that she was older than us—around Ray's age.

"These are so good," I said, ripping into the pretzels. "Maybe better than the pot."

Ray laughed. "Gotta stop competing with myself."

Kids said the draft board was doing a number on Ray: ridding the county of a "bad influence" and at the same time adding "a fine young man" to our armed forces. If that wasn't Orwellian doublespeak, I'd never heard it. Single, double, or any other speak, Vietnam was Vietnam.

Some kids thought Ray should go to Canada instead of Nam. But the draft dodgers could never come home, and how could anybody stand that?

"Hey, man, who's your date?" Andy asked.

"Meredith," she said, answering for herself.

Megan was holding several marshmallows over the flames as Dave sang, "Chestnuts roasting on an open fire. . . ."

Megan poked him. "Listen, male chauvinist pig"—her new term that she tried to use at least three times a day—"you're making me do all the cooking."

Meredith laughed. "Right on, sister."

"Now hold on theah, Stella," Dave drawled, drawing himself up. He'd been in Mr. Steig's lit class with me last year and we'd read *A Streetcar Named Desire.* "Jus' you rememah the Code Napoleon."

"Tell him what he can do with his code, hon," Meredith suggested to Megan.

Ray kicked a piece of wood into the fire with the tip of his boot. "I think y'all should know that my friend Meredith is an up-front women's libber, which, according to their rules of protocol, entitles her to wear those baubles, bangles, and beads you see on her ample bra-less bosom."

"Thus endeth the reading," someone murmured.

Meredith made a gesture I couldn't quite see, but when Ray laughed she put her arm around him and they sat down on some rocks and began to roll a joint.

They passed it around. When it came to me, I just gave it to Andy. I liked to get high, not stoned. Andy was playing with my hair, twisting it and brushing the tip lightly along my cheek. I stared into the embers. A log shifted and sent sparkles into the air.

"Let's go find some wood," Andy whispered, standing up.

I took his hand and gathered up the blanket. We seemed to float into the darkness.

"Back to where we were before we were so rudely interrupted," he murmured, pulling me down beside him, kissing me and sliding down the strap of my bathing suit. I wanted him to go on. This was love. It wasn't wrong. It was my body and I could do what I wanted with it.

Twigs crunched close by. Someone was walking nearer to us, breaking the rule that you *never* interrupted a couple who were making out. I touched Andy's hand, signaling him to stop.

A light played over us, then away, but not very far away.

I sat up, pulling my beach shirt closed. Andy put his arm over his face and made a sound of disgust.

I was looking into the face of Deputy Bill Byrd, younger brother of Dad's old friend Noah, who had been killed in the last war. The deputy was looking back, taking careful note of who I was.

I felt naked with embarrassment as Andy put his arm around me. What would happen? I stared at the buttons on the deputy's uniform; at the holster on his hip. Would I get hauled off to jail? Did he realize that I, personally, was not all that high and therefore not very guilty?

Dad would kill me even though I was practically innocent. Or this would kill him.

Deputy Byrd cleared his throat. "You kids get yourselves together."

Andy and I sat unmoving until we heard his voice over by the fire, talking to the others.

And then I dared to wipe the tears off my face and try to find the buttons on my shirt. "What will he do?" I whispered to Andy.

His voice shook a little. "If he doesn't find anything but pot on Ray, probably nothing much," he said.

My teeth chattered, despite the warmth of the August night, and Andy put the blanket over my shoulders.

At the fire, the deputy was kicking sand over the flames. "Everybody go on home now," he said.

I ran into the darkness, hoping nobody could hear me throwing up.

"Jim?" my mother called from her bedroom.

I pulled off my earphones. The blast of Jethro Tull had drowned out the usual screen-door thump of Dad's arrival.

"Dad's home." I bumped Mary Suzanne's shoulder with my hip as I passed the chaise where she'd been writing a letter to her fiancé, Tom.

"Hey, birthday girl," Dad said to me, appearing in the bedroom doorway. "Ready for the party?"

"Whadda you think?" I turned, modeling the new denim hip-huggers I'd had to lie down on the floor and use a coat hanger to zip.

He looked at me and tried not to shake his head, but it moved on its own. Yet when I smiled at him in the mirror, he smiled back.

"So how's my other pretty daughter? The one with the Ph.D.?" he asked, going for safer ground with Mary Suzanne.

"The old one," I said. My half-sister was twenty-seven. She'd been adopted by my dad and his first wife, Julia, on the eve of his going off to war. And Julia had died of cancer when Mary Suzanne was only seven years old.

"Good," she told him, ignoring me. "How's my scribble-meister father?"

"Jim." Mom's voice again.

Dad looked over his shoulder. "Let me find out what Alice wants."

I spritzed Tabu in the air, then twirled through it, making Mary Suzanne laugh.

"So who'd you invite for tonight?" she asked.

"Crissy and Megan, of course."

"Of course." Her expression didn't exactly change, but she knew that I knew she thought Crissy especially was bad news. She was right. Crissy *was* bad news. Crissy was *fun*. Same thing.

Dad was back. "C'mon, kids. Party's starting. Amos is here. Goodwins are here. Presents await." He had one of Mom's silk scarves in his hand.

Were we playing pin the tail on the donkey? Didn't Dad know I was *sixteen*—not six?

"I've got her," Mary Suzanne said, leaping off the chaise. "You blindfold her."

The scarf smelled like Mom's Joy perfume. That was ironic—that Mom, who felt so little joy, wore a perfume by that name. I let them lead me downstairs and out the front door. The brick walk was uneven, and I clung to Dad's arm.

He stopped. I felt Mary Suzanne behind me, untying the scarf. I sensed other people around me.

"Drum roll," Uncle Amos said.

Mary Suzanne whipped the scarf away.

At the curb was a new red VW Bug with a white ribbon on the windshield.

"Happy sixteenth, baby," Dad said, hugging me and kissing my head.

Mom was there, too, looking pretty in a sleeveless linen dress. I saw the signs of effort in her eyes as she clapped for me and then hugged me. "Happy birthday, sweetheart," she said.

"Happy birthday, kiddo," Uncle Amos said with a kiss.

"Wow." That's all I could say. "Wow."

"I think you popped out of the womb, looked at the bright lights, and said *wow*," Uncle Amos joked.

"I ordered you a new Caddy, girl. But when I heard Jim had got you a VW, I didn't want to hurt his feelings, so I canceled the order," Uncle Art teased.

Art Goodwin wasn't really my uncle. It was a courtesy title because he was Mary Suzanne's granddad. As he joked with me, he had his arm around her shoulders. They resembled each other—which was kind of funny, since Mary Suzanne was adopted.

In the excitement, Crissy and Megan had arrived and were in and out of the car like pop goes the weasel. Crissy threw her arms around me. "You are so lucky!" Then she whispered with a giggle, "We can have some high old times in that car."

I did a little dance around the VW and waved at Dad, who was watching me with a proud look on his face.

"Will I be able to get out, now that I'm in?" Mom worried, closing the passenger door on my little car.

She was taller than me, so her knees were pushed up against the dash. But she was having a good day, and I really wanted her to see how well I could drive with a stick shift. The car didn't have air-conditioning, so we rolled the windows down and Mom's silk scarf fluttered around her face.

"I used to drive a stick shift when I was a girl in New England. Downshifting is good for mountain roads." She went ahead to talk about her family's summer cabin and taking two girlfriends there for the whole of one summer. "I guess we were about sixteen then, like you are now."

I stopped at a light and was mentally rehearsing how to ease off the clutch and get going again without giving Mom whiplash, when she asked, "Are you happy being sixteen, Jill?"

I laughed, not wanting to spoil this rare carefree mood. "It's fine with me," I said. There was no point launching into the minutiae of my life. I knew Mom cared—in a general sort of way—but couldn't cope with the details.

In the A&P parking lot, soft tar patches over the asphalt cracks gave way underfoot. The Kiwanis were grilling hot dogs, and the smell made my mouth water. Mom glanced over that way, too.

"Maybe we could get something to eat in the car on the way home," she said.

I imagined biting down on the juicy hot dog, feeling the skin break beneath my teeth and the salty mustard tang fill my mouth. "Let's do that," I said.

She nodded, looking happy and energetic as she got her list out of her handbag. "Well, this may take a while, but that's okay, isn't it? It's a lovely day." As we went into the store, she said, "Doesn't the produce seem extra bright?"

The mounds of oranges, cabbages, and carrots appeared their normal selves to me, but I was glad to see her enjoying them.

"We'll cook the pot roast for Mary Suzanne with mushrooms and sherry," Mom decided. "And call the Goodwins and see if they'd like to join us."

Tonight was Mary Suzanne's last night before she went to teach her first term at Kent State. As Mary Suzanne got older, she and Mom related more as sort of distant sisters. Only recently had I realized that Mary Suzanne was as close to Mom's age as she was to mine.

"I'll go to the bakery section and see if they have angel food cakes," I offered, as Mom compared cartons of mushrooms.

She smiled, her blue eyes dancing with anticipation. "Wonderful. Why don't you get the frozen strawberries, too?"

When I came back with the cake and strawberries—which took a while because they were just putting out the cakes—Mom was standing in front of a mountainous display of iceberg lettuce. Somehow I could tell by her stiff posture that she'd been there a long time.

"I wonder if the produce manager has ever heard of endive? Or Bibb. Or cress. Or even romaine?" She looked at me, her eyes dull again. "Choices are nice."

Would Mom be happier if she had more choices? Did she ever want to get a job? But what would she do? She'd dropped out of Vassar to marry Dad when she was twenty and promptly had me.

We skipped the Kiwanian hot dogs, and Mom cried on the way home. I don't know what about. But it made my stomach hurt. "It's not got anything to do with you, Jill," she said, blowing her nose. "You have to understand that."

"I know," I said.

I managed to drive clear to our back door without jerking once and carried in the groceries. Mom went to her room. Mary Suzanne would be home in a while, and we could make the meal and invite her Goodwin grandparents over. It would still be nice.

The next day Mary Suzanne went off to Kent State, and the next week I returned to Jefferson High. Crissy, Megan, and I got in the habit of coming to my house in the afternoons.

Crissy dug around in the refrigerator. "Have I ever got the munchies!" She set out sour-cream dip and a square Tupperware container of celery sticks while I got the chips from the cupboard.

"Your mom's the only woman I've ever actually seen in a dressing gown," Megan whispered, getting a knife for the peanut butter. "Except in the movies."

Mom had just made her after-school appearance to my friends: a four o'clock vision—a little unreal, like Our Lady of Sorrows. And she now sat in the living room in a satin dressing gown the color of slightly softened butter. She seemed very mellow.

"I love the way she doesn't bug us." Crissy scooped up the sour cream on a chip and crammed it in her mouth, then she took a swig of pop. "Saved by the tiny bubbles."

Every day after school, we would pile in my car, drive out to this place we knew, share a roach, and then come here knowing there was no fear of getting busted, because my mother would be serene on the new tranquilizer the doctor had given her.

Crissy took another swig, standing with her eyes shut for a minute, then passed the can to me. I moved my fingers slightly on the pop can, picking up the little warm spots Crissy had left.

"You girls finding everything you need?" Mom called in a bright voice.

"Yes, thanks, Mrs. Snow," Crissy called back.

"Good." Mom drew out the word, her voice trailing off.

We were perfectly safe.

"I hear smoking pot can make you fat," Megan murmured, "because it increases your appetite."

Crissy hovered in mid-dip over the sour cream.

It better not make us fat, since it had been Crissy's idea in the first place, and she was always fretting about our weight.

"I read it somewhere just recently," Megan insisted, cutting little chunks of cheese for us.

"Where?" Crissy demanded.

"I think it was in a sidebar in the issue of *Marijuana Monthly* I picked up at the beauty shop." She snorted with laughter at the look on Crissy's face.

I held a warning finger to my lips. Too much laughter could be dangerous even when Mom was zoned out four rings from Saturn, as Mary Suzanne said.

"You've never been in a beauty shop in your life," I told Megan. She was the school knockout.

Crissy and I had been best friends all last year, but only this summer had Megan drifted away from her cheerleading practice and the homecoming queen crowd into our new threesome and taken on the charge of radicalizing us.

We took our munchies and pop out onto the sun porch, and I raised some windows, making the breeze riffle the pages of *Mademoiselle* magazine on the coffee table. Megan arranged herself on a chaise.

Crissy curled up in an easy chair. "Seriously, I have heard birth-control pills can make you fat."

Megan and I glanced at each other. In the hierarchy of secret things we carried in our purses, Crissy's birth-control pills trumped everything. The little stores of marijuana. The ceramic roach clips that Megan's brother had brought us from Mexico. Tampax.

There was the rumble of the garage door going up.

Dad! What was he doing home so early?

We scrambled, straightening pillows, slipping into our shoes, composing our faces. We did everything but true up the cheese squares on our crackers as we heard Dad's entry into the kitchen.

"Hello, girls," he said, coming out to the sun porch. "How was school?"

We smiled. *Fine. Great. Really excellent, Mr. Snow. Did you have a good day? What are you doing home so early?* We sounded like a little flock of sparrows coming in for a nervous landing.

I watched Dad's face. He'd recently written a couple of editorials that showed he was more on top of our counterculture experiment right here in Jefferson-by-God, Iowa, than I'd thought. But all I saw was his usual affectionate tolerance.

Chapter Two

LEANING AGAINST the foyer wall, I tugged on my boots.

"You're gonna need those," Dad said, coming down the stairs. "It's a snowy night."

I peered out the long window beside the door into the twilight. It *was* snowing, but did Dad really think I'd wear *snow boots*, like some old lady? And maybe one of those clear plastic bonnets to keep my hair-sprayed helmet-hard coiffure from getting wet?

I hummed "These Boots Are Made for Walkin'" as I pulled the soft forest-green suede up over my calves. They made a statement.

"Snow's early this year," Dad mused. "If it falls much with so many leaves still on, we'll get downed trees. We could have a power failure. You have all your homework done? Be hard to do it in the dark."

"Would I be going out if I didn't?" I asked, kissing him on the cheek. Technically, that was a question, not a lie.

"Where are you going?" He looked at his watch. "It's about dinnertime."

Of late, Dad seemed more watchful of me. Had he heard something about me or my friends?

"We're just gonna grab some food and head straight for the library."

That was a lie, not a question, and I regretted it. But we were only going to pick up some kids and ride around in Crissy's dad's big Dodge four-door.

"I wish you'd eat here a little more often," Dad said. Something in his voice seemed carping.

"C'mon, Dad," I said, turning on my best smile, "I'm sixteen, remember?"

I don't think my smile worked the voodoo it usually did. His expression flickered, and he just nodded. "Working on a big school project?"

"Yep. Mr. Steig."

Dad nodded again. He knew I liked Mr. Steig's class. Not only was Mr. Steig smart, he understood us. And he had us do things that actually required thinking. *And* he was gorgeous.

I pulled on my fringed suede jacket and glanced at myself in the hallway mirror. If Dad hadn't been standing there, I'd have checked my posture from several angles and maybe tugged a strand of hair loose so it hung in a sexy curl at the side.

I had my hand on the doorknob. Crissy wasn't here yet, but I'd just walk down the sidewalk and enjoy the snow. Get out of the house.

"Jill," Dad asked, "do you know Ray Miller?"

So that was it.

I hung on to the doorknob and made myself count to three before I turned around. "I know who he is."

"They say he's gone to Canada to avoid the draft." I didn't quite understand the expression on Dad's face. "It must be hard for a boy to do that."

I shut my eyes, letting out my breath, giddy with relief. Dad didn't know after all. My shameful first thought was to wonder where we'd get our stuff now. Ray had a younger brother named Glen, about my age, but he seemed more into chorus than cash crops.

"You know he can never come back," Dad said. "Imagine leaving your home forever."

I heard the sound of Mom's six o'clock TV program coming from her room and smelled the stuffed pork chops our twice-a-week housekeeper, Norma, had put in the oven. I'd lived in this house with its winding oak staircase and stained-glass window on the landing my whole life. I tried to think about never being here again, and I felt ill.

"Yeah," I said. "It sucks."

Dad blinked and swallowed hard at the word. "Some of the steps you young people take so heedlessly scare me," he finally said.

Avoiding Nam was hardly "heedless," but how could I argue, especially when I agreed that just the thought of leaving home gave me the creeps? Dad walked with a slight limp because he had been wounded on Leyte in 1945. I'd found his purple heart in a memento box one day and had asked Mom about it.

But that had been a whole different war.

Dad gave me everything I wanted *and* felt bad that the neighborhood drug dealer could never come home again. I probably didn't deserve him.

I was starting to unbutton my jacket. Maybe I should stay home tonight after all. It wouldn't kill me. Just then, though, Crissy tooted out front and the phone rang at the same time.

"That'll be Mary Suzanne," Dad said, turning to the phone. She called every Wednesday night at six o'clock. "You have fun. Get your work done and head home before the roads turn bad. No later than nine thirty, okay?"

Crissy honked again.

What should I do?

I looked in the mirror. I looked good. It would be a shame to waste it.

"Okay," I told Dad.

Megan pulled a face when I got in beside her and Crissy.

"You look crabby," she said, as Crissy headed for the Burger Barn. "Are you?"

"No." I sighed. "He just doesn't understand."

"That would be your dad?" Crissy said. "He doesn't like your tight jeans and wants you to eat absolutely every meal in the bosom of your family, right?"

"Sort of."

Crissy nodded. "He seems pretty nice to me. I like your dad."

"Yeah," I said. "And there's one other thing." I told them about Ray.

"That's a crock!" Megan exploded. "The powers-that-be tell the guy, 'You've got to fight in our despicable, immoral war, and if you bug out for Canada, you'd better not come back 'cause we'll getcha.'"

"Right," I said.

Crissy pulled into a parking place at the Burger Barn. I could smell the grease before we opened the car doors.

"Cheer up, sisters," Crissy said. "Hey, do you know what they call rock 'n' roll in German?"

I bit. "What?"

"Rock *und* roll."

It wasn't funny, but it made me feel better.

Monday morning, Mr. Steig stopped me as Crissy and I were coming out of history class. As she walked on, Crissy rolled her eyes and gave me a goofy smile. To have Mr. Steig talk to you in the hall was a rush.

"The student activities committee wants a skit on freedom of speech for the Thanksgiving assembly. I need somebody to put it together," he told me.

"That's only two days off."

"We're not looking for *Hamlet* here. They were going to have that lady from the Daughters of the American Revolution do a little program, but she's in the hospital. We only need a ten-minute filler on current freedom issues. Between when the band plays and when Mr. Carruthers gives his usual Thanksgiving speech," he went on. "You probably wouldn't need more than three or four short parts."

I wanted to make a good impression on Mr. Steig. "Okay," I said. "I'll do it."

Drama class was the last period of the day. As the radiator hissed and pinged and Mr. Steig explained the project and that I would "direct" it—which made me sit up a little straighter—I saw Andy offering a Chiclet to Jana, his new chicklette. I watched the way their fingers touched as they tried to get the little white square from his box to her hand without making distracting noises. I saw the way he smiled right into her eyes.

Too bad for me, I guess. He'd been calling less and less, and he made clear he expected a chick to put out, which I didn't plan to do—despite what he might have thought from that one night on the beach last summer when I was kind of high. So it was probably *Good-bye, Andy.*

For the skit, he managed to get Mr. Steig to allow him to make a short speech on legalizing marijuana. The kids in the audience would eat it up.

Carla would speak on women's economic rights, and Megan would speak against the war in Vietnam. We needed one more.

"I got it," Jana said. "I'll have my mom drape me in a gown like that Columbia movie woman, and I'll hold a torch."

No one could deny she was statuesque. "And . . ." Mr. Steig prompted.

"Well, my speech will say that my body is my own to do with as I wish, and my torch lights the way to acceptance of my right."

There was a peppering of applause from the guys, though the speech sounded kind of scary to me.

Mr. Steig nodded.

So on the Wednesday morning before Thanksgiving, a half dozen of us were excused from our classes to get things set up and to squeeze in a rehearsal.

I had on black hip-huggers and a black turtleneck and, despite the icy wood floor, had left off my shoes as a political statement. Mary Suzanne told me she'd worn a little black dress, pearls, and bare feet to a faculty party on Tom's campus in September. Bare feet were a small sign of freedom, she said, though I didn't totally understand how.

I'd also ironed my hair, so it made a straight, long curtain over my shoulders, and I'd put on lots of eyeliner. I looked like a director should look.

I positioned my stool at stage left, where I would sit and narrate the appearance of "The Four New Freedoms," which was what we'd titled the skit.

Becky had unfolded a ladder and set in front of it a painted prop of the bodies of downtrodden women workers. She'd talked Andy into going up the ladder as she declared women's freedom from oppression in the workplace.

I tried not to smirk at the idea of Andy as both sexual oppressor and pot freedom rider in the same skit.

Then Mr. Steig came across the stage toward me. "Jill, we have a problem."

He noticed my bare feet and rolled his eyes.

"We sure do," Megan added, fast on his heels. "Jana's really sick. She puked on the bass drum in the band room and went home." She lifted her hands to me in a so-what'cha-gonna-do gesture.

I wished we'd titled the skit just "The Freedoms." Then nobody would have known one had fallen. Other than Mr. Steig, I was the only person familiar with all the parts. And he could hardly speak for the freedom of women to do what they wanted with their bodies. He could take on the role of narrator, though. I had everything all typed out.

I didn't like where this was headed.

A few minutes later, I held Jana's free-love speech in my hand and was glad the room had no mirror. My sophisticated black director's garb lay in a pitiful pile under a music stand. I wore a bedsheet and carried a cardboard torch.

I watched from the wings as the gym filled. From the floor, the band played "God Bless America," and then we were on.

The curtain went up on Megan, who stood on her soapbox, her arms at her side, clutching her speech. Probably the audience couldn't see it, but I could tell her legs were shaking. Her voice wavered at the beginning, but then it grew strong as she talked about what was wrong with the war and about our right to express our feelings.

She got good applause at the end, though I saw a couple of kids in the back stand up and cup their hands into a boo. A teacher motioned for them to sit down.

When the curtain went up on Andy, there was a riff of laughter. Whatever Andy said, the kids knew it would be funny. Although the teachers who stood along the back wall of the gym probably thought he was a little outrageous, applause pounded when he was done.

The curtain dropped and came up again on Carla,

whose appeal for women's equal rights in the workplace was ardent, and Andy mugged the male oppressor role just enough to get oceans of applause at the end. For the first time in a while, I really liked Andy again.

I would have given him a smile as he came offstage, except I couldn't move my lips. How would I ever be able to read Jana's speech about free love?

"Go," Mr. Steig said, touching my shoulder. "You're on."

The curtain went up. I looked at the audience and took a breath, my torch high, readying myself. I let out my breath, like I'd been trained to do in drama class. I connected with the faces, then took another breath to begin. And that's when I saw my dad, standing in the back of the gymnasium.

Jana's typewritten script shook in my hands. I botched the beginning, actually saying "buddies" for "bodies." What was Dad doing here? What was he thinking of me? Would I never, ever get to the end?

I parked in front of the hardware store and ran across the street to the newspaper office. The wind blew open my jacket, and the sky had the dullness of a coming storm. The place looked empty even though it was only noon.

"Hello?" I called, the door rattling shut behind me. "Dad?"

His voice came from the back. "File room."

I found him at a table wedged into a forest of four-drawer metal cabinets. The smell of coffee that had been in the percolator all morning clung to the air. "Where is every-body?"

"Marian wanted to start her Thanksgiving cooking. Tom is over at the hospital interviewing the farmer who fell in his grain bin. I don't know where Pete is."

His hair shone silver against the gloomy light. He looked tired.

"I got a 98 on my physics test," I told him, hoping for a smile.

"Well, I know you didn't inherit that talent from me."

I cleared a chair of dusty notebooks and sat down. Was he mad at me? Could we just ignore the whole thing?

"I had to get my talent from somewhere," I said, feeling the need to talk to Dad—about anything.

He seemed to be thinking about it. "Probably your Grandpa Snow," he offered eventually. "They used to call him Sparky because he could take apart and put together a car engine as easy as most men can cut up and eat their pork chop. Never went to high school."

I hadn't known either of my Snow grandparents. They'd died before I was born. "Why didn't he go to high school?" I asked.

He shrugged, playing with a paper clip. "Different times, I guess."

Dad's mood felt as gloomy as the weather. I wished Mary Suzanne were coming home for Thanksgiving, but she was going to Case Western Reserve to spend it with Tom. Mom would try to go through the motions, but it would be grim. Maybe I could talk Crissy and Megan into driving down to Des Moines on Friday to shop.

"You probably have work to do. I guess I should go." But I really didn't want to go. I'd been pushing Dad away from me for several months, and the thought that I might have succeeded made me ill.

"Dad, are you mad at me?" I felt tears come on the question mark.

He looked at me for a long time, tapping the paper clip against the table, running it through his fingers, turning it, tapping it again. Finally, he shook his head.

"Good. Because I haven't done anything wrong, you know." I really hadn't.

He lowered his head a little and raised one eyebrow.

It was chilly in the file room, despite the hissing radiator. I slouched in the chair, putting my hands in my coat pocket. My fingers touched the roach clip, which was usually in my purse. My eyes flicked to Dad's. He was looking at me in such a searching way.

Was he looking for the skinny little girl he could pick up and hold and make her owies go away?

"Did the skit upset you?" I asked.

He put the paper clip back in the little dish. "I was expecting to hear Mildred Pearson talking about the DAR," he said. "So I was surprised to see you up there—" He broke off.

"Oh God, Dad." I put my hand over my face. "The body speech wasn't even mine. Jana wrote it and was supposed to do it. Then, just before the assembly, she got sick. I was her stand-in."

"So you don't believe any of that crap?" he asked.

"Well . . ."

"The antiwar protests, legalizing marijuana, the women's libber stuff?"

He was pushing me.

"Well yeah, I believe some of it. It doesn't seem right to make boys go to Vietnam. They didn't start the war." Megan said old men started the war—that that was the way it always was. Old men capitalists started it, then kids had to actually fight it.

"And pot is no worse than the drinking and smoking of your generation," I pointed out. Surely he could see that.

"But it's *illegal*," he said. "You could go to jail for it. I couldn't help you."

"Oh, Dad . . ."

"Jill, I hear things."

A thread of fear tightened. Had Deputy Byrd, the one who'd busted us on the beach before school started, said something to Dad?

Did he think I was exercising my God-given right to screw whoever I wanted to, as Jana said? Well, I wasn't. And I wished I could tell Dad that, but of course I couldn't.

He pushed a piece of paper across the desk. "Editorial" was typed at the top, with "Have You Noticed?" centered under that. "Have you noticed our children, our Greene County, Iowa, children? The headbands. The scruffy clothes. Many are dirty. They have sources for drugs. They don't like the war in Vietnam. Well, many of us don't either. They tell us to listen to their celebrity protest leaders. Hayden, the Berrigans, Hoffman (who is kind of funny), people who are against everything and in favor of nothing. And they talk to us about 'free love.'"

He'd stopped writing there.

"Jill, I can neither finish that nor print it if I did finish it because you're one of those children."

"I'm not *dirty*." I washed my hair every day. What did Dad think I was doing in the bathroom for hours? I lived in front of the mirror. And I had a closet full of clothes that our housekeeper washed every week. "I'm not a child either!"

"Yes, *you are!*" It was the closest he'd ever come to yelling at me. We were both stunned.

"Dad . . ."

But I didn't have anything to say. He looked, but he wasn't seeing me. He saw the ratty kids who hung around the square, kids who were into stuff a lot worse than I was. He saw kids on television, young men and women, really, who rioted in the streets and shot heroin. Dad equated a little pot to what he imagined. I should have just gone out to Spring Lake with Crissy and Megan rather than coming here and trying to talk to him.

Mary Suzanne held up a fringed velvet scarf. "Alice might like this."

"Maybe." The scarf was beautiful, but Mom hardly ever went out, and she had drawers and drawers of beautiful things. I'd like to give her something that truly made her happy.

"I wish we'd gone down to Des Moines," I said. The Penney's store—though it was the zenith of shopping in Jefferson—didn't really have much.

"In this weather?" Mary Suzanne said. "I'm just glad I flew home yesterday instead of today."

Looking out the arched windows beyond ladies' wear, I saw fat snow tumbling out of a thick sky. "You're right. I hope Megan and Crissy and everybody stay on the road."

Mary Suzanne continued with her scarf search. "Where'd they go?"

"To one of Megan's war protests in Ames."

"I'm surprised you're not with them. Dad says you're really getting into all that."

"Oh, *Dad*. He doesn't know—" I broke off with a shake of my head. But the truth was, I'd stayed home because of him. To make him see that my friends could go off and I didn't have to go with them. I wanted him to know that I really was just as he wanted me to be. Almost, anyway.

Please, Megan had begged, throwing her arms around me in her wildly dramatic way. *It'll be totally peaceful. We'll just sit down and link arms. We need everybody we can get.* Which had turned out to be just Crissy, Andy, and Jana. I hadn't been able to come up with a good reason for not going, and Megan had been pissed. I hated choosing between Dad and my friends.

"Everything here seems so *boring*," I told Mary Suzanne, looking around at the scarves, gloves, costume jewelry, and cologne. "What did you get my mom?"

"Mosaic earrings. I'll have to show them to you. They came from Greece. I got them at the Christmas bazaar at the Unitarian church."

"Kent must be exotic." In Jefferson we had mainly the Methodist church. And nothing at all from Greece.

Mary Suzanne laughed. "Kent is the blandest place east of the Mississippi, as I was telling Dad. One or two Unitarians and a couple of college students who claim to belong to the Students for a Democratic Society."

I gazed over the store—sparkly blouses, a BED AND BATH LINENS sign, a huge plastic snowflake hanging from the ceiling. There was nothing here that would make my mother happy.

"Let's go to Haas's and have Dutch letters," I said. "I'm hungry."

Outside, the wind drove the snow horizontally. I put my hand over my face, but flakes still blew on my neck and melted, trickling down inside my coat.

Inside the bakery, the delicious spicy smells made me half dizzy. Maybe I could cook Mom something for Christmas. Something truly wonderful, like the crème brûlée I'd had at the Tea Room in Des Moines. Or a baked Alaska. At least she would eat it and it would be gone—not just end up in her graveyard closet with all the other stuff.

When we'd settled in by the window with our almond-paste-filled goodies, Mary Suzanne picked up our conversation from earlier. "About Dad," she began.

I looked away, watching a car slide at the stop sign.

"He's having trouble dealing with some of your attitudes, Jill. Remember, when he was your age, many of the roads weren't even paved."

Here came the I'm-your-big-sister-and-I-understand-things-better-than-you-do lecture.

"I've heard about that a million times. How he and Aunt Cathy and their parents went on a road trip to Colorado. I wonder why Aunt Cathy never comes to Jefferson?" I mused, making a blatant effort to change the subject away from Dad.

Mary Suzanne said, "She *did* come for Grandfather Snow's funeral. And Grandmother's, too. I was little, but I remember. And I remember that both times, she was pregnant. And my mom and Aunt Cathy wrote to each other all the time. Did you know that? Mom used to send her pictures of me. And Mom and Dad and I went to see her once. Aunt Cathy lived in a big old Southern mansion behind curtains of Spanish moss. She was married to a doctor. Dr. Henry Devereaux."

"What was your mother like?" I asked. Thinking of Dad married to a woman other than Mom was weird.

"Wonderful. Did you know I never knew I was adopted until after she died? Dad told me about a year later. He said I was getting big and needed to know. That I might hear it from somebody else someday, and he wanted to tell me first."

"You look so much like the Goodwins and the Snows," I marveled. "It's amazing."

She laughed. "Probably because I thought I *was* a Goodwin and a Snow for the first ten years of my life. Environment versus heredity."

Outside the window, I saw Carla in her red and orange plaid coat. Head down, she clutched the hood to keep the wind from grabbing it. I tapped on the window and waved when she looked up. Her eyes were huge and dark.

She rushed into the bakery, sliding in the slushy entryway. "Oh, Jill! Have you heard? They got into a wreck!"

"Who?" I stood up, sloshing our coffee. "Who got into a wreck?"

"Andy and them. Crissy's hurt bad. They're taking her to Iowa Methodist Hospital in Des Moines."

The Dutch letter threatened to come back up.

"Oh, Jill, what if she dies?" Carla's voice wavered as she reached for me.

My best friend, Crissy, who always knew where to find fun and mischief? My heart seemed to stall. "Tell me everything."

Carla's fingers trembled as she turned back her hood. "Well, the others are hurt. But not so bad. That's all I know. Except it happened just this side of Grand Junction, and Rusty Phillips came by the scene to help and . . ." She lowered her voice. "And maybe Andy was stoned."

I shut my eyes for a minute, then opened them as I felt the terror of what the wreck might have been like for my friends.

"It could have been me," Carla said. "I'd have gone if I hadn't had to work."

I stood up and hugged her, her ice-crusted hood stinging my cheek. I'd have gone, too, if it hadn't been for Dad.

Dad personally covered the accident, getting to the scene before they had managed to pry Crissy loose from the wreckage. He came home white as death, his limp so pronounced he seemed to lurch. Mom poured him a big shot of whiskey and had him lie on the couch and put his feet up on the armrest. Lying there, his feet elevated as we all fussed around him, he stared at me in a way I didn't understand. But his look scared me.

As soon as Crissy was out of intensive care, I went to see her down in Des Moines. There were so many bandages, tubes, cords, racks, and beeping things that I could hardly find her blue eyes, and when I did we both started to cry. Her jaws were wired shut, and she was dopey from pain medication. Later, out in the corridor, her mom told me Crissy would need several surgeries and months of physical therapy.

Megan—beautiful Megan—returned to school the last day before Christmas vacation with a deep gash on her forehead closed with dark Frankenstein stitches.

That same day, Andy found me alone in the drama room and swore on a volume of Shakespeare that he hadn't been stoned when the accident happened. That in fact he'd been stone-cold *sober* because he was so wimpy about driving on icy roads. We were all beginning drivers, without much experience, and I hugged Andy and patted his back while he cried.

I went through the holidays with my stomach either hurting or feeling like it was going to jump out of my mouth. Wrapping packages and putting up the tree seemed impossible. For the first time ever, I understood why Mom sometimes just went to bed and didn't want to get up.

The day after Christmas, I stayed in my bedroom with the door closed, eating only the stash of pretzels and M&M's in my nightstand and listening to Bob Dylan. I kept the curtains pulled and burned incense and hoped everybody would leave me alone.

The sounds of Dad and Mom and Mary Suzanne moving around sometimes came through the music, but not much. I thought about taking a shower and getting out of my baggy peace-sign T-shirt that I'd slept in, but what was the point?

In the afternoon, somebody knocked on my door, and Dad opened it before I turned down the music. "Let's go for a walk," he said in his no-nonsense tone.

I shrugged, not wanting him to know how much I hated the way things were between us. But maybe he did know. Maybe that's why he wanted us to take a walk together.

"Let me get dressed," I said. I pulled on a pair of frayed bell-bottoms and a turtleneck.

Dad was standing in the foyer waiting when I got downstairs, his jacket already on. He was staring out the narrow window with his hands in his pockets.

He held the door open for me, and I bit back a comment I might have made when things were easier between us, about how guys didn't do that anymore because it was patronizing.

The blast of fresh air made me feel better. Gutters were dripping with a midwinter thaw. I didn't even button my pea coat.

We saw hardly anybody—just a group of kids shooting baskets in front of a garage. After a couple of blocks, the sun went behind a cloud, taking all the warmth out of the day. Dad was still limping more than usual.

"Jill, I want to talk to you."

I wanted to talk to him, too. To explain things. The accident two weeks ago had slowed us all down. But maybe it could be an occasion for making things right. I would ease off the antiwar politics. All the fire had gone out of Megan anyway. I had decided my body was indeed mine to do what I wanted with, but so far I hadn't met anybody who seemed deserving of the honor—though I would never go into all that with Dad.

The cloud blew over and the sun streamed down again and I turned my face up to it. Crissy would eventually get better and we'd be together—having fun, smoking a little pot, but coming in closer to home.

We'd gotten too near the fire.

"I've talked to Mary Suzanne," Dad said. "She's agreed that you can go back to Kent with her and go to high school there. At least for the second semester. Then we'll see."

I stopped. "But—"

"No buts," Dad said, walking on so I had to trot to catch up.

"But, Dad—" I tugged on his arm.

He stopped finally, turning to face me. "I cannot trust you to do what you ought to do, to be where you ought to be, to have good friends. And I'm not going to take any more chances. Mary Suzanne says Kent is a nice town and you can start over with new friends there."

"But, Dad, I'll do it here. We were all getting a little carried away, maybe."

"So carried away your friend Crissy nearly died when that manic boy loaded on God knows what lost control of the car. And you were almost with them." His voice rose on the last sentence and I felt Dad could have actually hit me, which he'd never, ever done.

"He wasn't loaded, Dad." I tried to keep my voice reasonable. "He swore to me. He just didn't know how to drive on icy roads."

But Dad's face was closed, and I knew I may as well stop talking.

Dad's shoulders lowered, and we began walking again. "I won't have you in harm's way, Cathy," he muttered, almost to himself.

"Jill," I said.

He looked at me, his face racing through expressions I didn't understand. If he sent me away, I'd die.

Chapter Three

WE DROVE MY VW to Kent, leaving early. The day was drab, with old, dirty snow. Mary Suzanne didn't have much to say, and I wondered if she was already sorry she'd let Dad talk her into this.

My good-bye with Mom had been teary. With Dad it had been stony-faced and curt.

Even if I returned in the summer, nothing would be the same with me and my friends. And I held Dad responsible for that.

Crossing the Mississippi River really bugged me. *Good-bye, Iowa,* I said to myself as Mary Suzanne drove over the big span. The names of the towns on the highway exit signs—Peoria, Chicago, Indianapolis—seemed to drop like an axe, chopping off little parts of who I was.

Twilight was settling as we drove into Kent from the west. A huge, pink moon rose in the east.

"Why is the moon pink?" I asked.

"Pollution," Mary Suzanne answered.

I thought of the wonderful silver moons over Spring Lake. "Moons shouldn't *be* pink."

Finally, as we bounced over railroad tracks in downtown Kent, Mary Suzanne remarked, "It seems kind of deserted now because most of the students have gone home over Christmas."

Actually, it looked like the Andromeda Strain had swept through.

Across the street from a darkened fraternity house, Mary Suzanne turned up a steep gravel drive. A huge old house loomed at the top, lights showing in part of it.

"A guy from Ireland rents half, and I rent the other," she explained.

Carrying an armload of clothes on hangers, I followed her and waited while she struggled to find the keyhole in the darkness. She flicked on a harsh overhead light and held the door open.

A kitchen table sat in front of windows that were partially iced in the corners. I didn't know where else to put my clothes, so I just laid them on the table. I heard Mary Suzanne walking around. The place smelled musty.

"Let's get you unloaded," Mary Suzanne said briskly, reappearing.

I swallowed my homesickness.

We trekked back and forth, unpacking the things I'd crammed in the front trunk of the VW. By our last trip, warm air had begun to whoosh from the heat registers.

"This will be where you stay when we get you a bed," she said, turning on the light in a room at the top of a flight of steep stairs. The sloping ceiling under the roofline made the room seem even smaller than it was. And it was crammed with books, wooden file cabinets, Mary Suzanne's desk, and an easy chair with a footstool. It was about a tenth the size of my bedroom back home.

"Where will you put your stuff?" I asked.

"There's a little sleeping porch off my bedroom down-stairs. I can use that for a study. I have some football players in my comp class. After school starts, I'll get them over to move furniture."

From a dormer window, I looked down on Main Street far below. A siren in the distance made me think of Crissy lying in a hospital room with machines humming and beeping around her.

"Are you hungry?" Mary Suzanne asked.

Usually I was starving, but now I wasn't. "Not much," I said.

"Well, let's see what's in the refrigerator anyway, then call Alice and Dad and let them know we got here."

I tended the bacon and eggs while she called. I shook my head when she put her hand over the receiver and said

Dad wanted to talk to me. I ran water in the hissing skillet so I didn't have to hear her explain to him why I wouldn't come to the phone.

Later, we made me a bed on the couch, and Mary Suzanne went into her room and shut the door. I lay on the couch, my body stiff and rigid under the neatly turned-back blanket. A bright streetlight came through the floor-to-ceiling windows. I was still vibrating from the long road trip. I had a little stash of pot in my purse, which would relax me, but the thought of smoking it without my friends made me squeeze my eyes shut.

During the next few days, we cleared out the upstairs room of all Mary Suzanne's things, hauling several boxes of files to her office on campus. She gave me a tour of the building, and then we walked by some empty dormitories and through the deserted Student Union.

On the first day of school, the dawn was a pure, promising blue. Mary Suzanne had asked a graduate student to cover her morning lit class so she could register me.

"I feel so old," she said, unplugging the coffee pot and pulling on her coat. "Like I have a high-school-aged daughter."

"You don't look old." Actually, she looked really pretty, in a matching skirt and V-neck sweater, her long reddish blond hair tied back with a scarf. "How do I look?" I'd spent over an hour trying to get myself just right. If I had to be here, I may as well try.

"Amazing," Mary Suzanne said with a smile, taking in my faded jeans and serape.

By lunch time, I'd discovered the kids were friendly enough.

Lena Fisher, whose dad taught in the English department with Mary Suzanne, found me at lunch and introduced herself.

"My dad says your dad is the publisher of a newspaper."

I kept a smile on my face, but I flinched inside at the mention of Dad. "Yeah. Back home."

"Are you interested in journalism? Do you think you'd like to work on the school paper?"

"I did, back home." I had to stop saying *back home*. It was starting to sound like the Shire in Middle Earth.

"Well, I'll introduce you to Mr. Delving, then. He's the journalism teacher. He encourages us to delve deeply."

I made the obligatory groan as I finished my Fritos. Maybe Mr. Delving would be like Mr. Steig, the faculty hunk in horn-rimmed glasses.

But he wasn't. He was average height and width with average coloring and pictures of very average-looking children on his desk.

"So how would you like to have the university campus beat?" he asked after we'd chatted for a while. "A lot of our high school students end up going to college there, so we try to keep it in the paper."

"But I've only set foot on the campus once, when I went with my sister to move some things into her office."

"Then you'll have an outsider's view, which is always more objective," he said.

"Okay. I'd like to."

After school, Lena offered me a ride. I could have walked, because it was only about seven blocks, but I said sure. Getting in her car made me think of Crissy and Megan. There I went again. *Back home.* Megan must be dying of loneliness.

I wished Lena was really a friend instead of just a friendly person I'd met at noon.

By late March, little clumps of scrubby grass were trying their best to turn green. Running up the front steps, I grabbed our mail out of the box before I went inside, and then I ran back down the steps and picked a few crocuses that were growing at the edge of the sidewalk. "I'm back," I called, "bearing water crackers and crocuses."

There was a letter from Megan in the mail.

Afternoon light fell through the front windows, and the apartment smelled of baking brie.

"Well done, half-sibling," Mary Suzanne said, rushing out of the kitchen barefooted and wearing a long skirt. She had her hair brushed so it all hung over one shoulder. "People will be here soon." She began to open the package of water crackers. "Oh, crocuses. Nice. Put them in a bowl and get some music going."

"In a minute. I want to read what Megan has to say."

Mary Suzanne was having an open house for some faculty and students. She told me I could invite friends, too, but even after three months I didn't really have any *friend* friends.

Megan wrote that Crissy was out of the hospital and going to Des Moines for rehab. She probably wouldn't be returning to school this year. She wondered if it could really be as dull as I said in my new high school. Was there any SDS activity in Kent?

When the doorbell rang and I opened the door, a woman pressed a dish of something warm into my hands and demanded that I call her Miriam. "And this is George Andwell." She introduced a man with hair longer than Mary Suzanne's that fell over his shoulders in silver and gray waves. "Sometimes known as Dr. And/Or."

George Andwell. "George Orwell," I said, proud of myself for getting it. And/Or.

"Mary Suzanne has a keeper here," the man said, hugging my shoulders. His gray tweed jacket was scratchy, and he reeked of pot.

"Jill, will you get the phone?" Mary Suzanne called from the kitchen.

It was Dad. I was glad the apartment was filling with noise and I could tell him it was a bad time. The truth was, every time I heard his voice was a bad time, and I always cried despite my clench-jawed resolve not to. There was something so wrong between us that I couldn't even think about it.

"Well, I'll get right to it," he said. I could hear the disappointment. "Your mother and I were hoping you and Mary Suzanne would come home for spring break."

I had the perfect excuse all ready. "The high school break isn't the same time as Mary Suzanne's. And I know you wouldn't want me driving alone."

I could tell by the silence that he felt both the dig and the readiness of my answer. I bit my lip, sorry and not sorry to hurt him.

"Then we could come out and see you."

Oh, no. That would be worse. It would probably end up being just Dad.

"Jill . . ." I heard the rawness in his voice. Was *he* crying? He never cried. "Look. We'd really like to come."

Mary Suzanne was stuck listening to one of her students, and the doorbell rang again.

"The open house is picking up speed, Dad. We'll call you Wednesday night. Gotta go."

Somebody else opened the door, so I had a second to collect myself and wipe away the tears. Dad was like God or oxygen. Just there. I didn't have the logic or the words or the *reason* to deal with the loss.

The apartment filled up fast.

One of the faculty with a preppy haircut started bugging Dr. And/Or about his long locks.

"The campus was with you last year, Mel," Dr. And/Or said, laughing. "Short hair to go with their short memories of anything academic."

Another kid standing there who didn't look a lot older than me, with a bush of curly blond hair, said, "Yeah, things are different this year. Maybe not academically. But the SDS is on campus now."

Ah. I could report that to Megan.

Dr. And/Or put his arm around me. "Jill, meet John Harker. Our best and brightest undergraduate English major."

The blond-haired boy stepped close. "Please, you'll jinx me," he said to Dr. And/Or before he told me what a good teacher Mary Suzanne was. Then he returned to the argument with Miriam over whether the growing unrest was really about Vietnam.

He reminded me of Megan with his intensity. Even his good looks, his fair hair, and blue eyes were like hers. I wondered if her Frankenstein scar had healed.

John must have wondered why I was looking at him like that—what I was thinking.

"Say, you should come over to our place sometime," he said. "You can meet my girlfriend, Wanda, and hang out with us."

I nodded. Something about John felt familiar, as if I might have found a real friend here at last.

Chapter Four

By about four thirty on Friday afternoon I'd finished making the changes Mr. Delving wanted to my article on summer freshman orientation activities. As I walked toward Mary Suzanne's apartment, the late-afternoon air was warm. Budding trees stood out against a blue and pink May sky.

Downtown, the bars thudded with music and students overflowed onto the sidewalk, carrying the aroma of beer and pot with them.

As I walked through the crowd on Water Street, a skinny guy handed me a just-budding sprig of lilacs. "Peace, babe." He had a whole armful of branches, as if he'd hacked down a bush.

"Peace," I said, taking the blossoms and holding them to my face as I walked on up the hill. The sky itself had turned a serene lilac color. Somebody had spray-painted OUT OF CAMBODIA on the sidewalk.

At the apartment, I changed clothes and left a note for Mary Suzanne telling her I was going over to John and Wanda's place. I had known them for over a month now. Back outside, I smelled somebody's cookout and felt a rush of hunger. Maybe Wanda would have some of her famous brownies.

The Delta Tau Delta's house had a keg in the front yard. A plastic cup flipped in the breeze and rolled down the lawn, off the retaining wall, across the sidewalk in front of me, and into the street, where it got caught in a stream of water and carried away.

A couple of fraternity guys were clambering out an upstairs window onto the roof of the porch, lugging a brown couch with them. "Hey!" one of them yelled, waving to me.

"Hey!" I called back.

A few houses down, a girl screamed, "I'll get you, asshole!" Her hair dripped and she flicked water off her hands. As a boy ran after her with a surging garden hose, she fled through the hedge into the next yard.

Oblivious to the water fight, a couple sat on a retaining wall at the end of the block, their feet on dusty duffels. They had look-alike long, frizzy hair and mumbled something to me.

A group of kids fled down the hill. As they got close, they split, some cutting across a yard and others darting into the street. Cars honked, and one of the kids pounded on a hood and yelled, "Pig!"

And there I stood, suddenly face-to-face with a gang of guys holding water balloons.

"Not me," I cried. "Not me."

They hesitated. Couldn't they tell that since I wasn't running I wasn't one of the group they were chasing?

Then one of them let loose a rebel yell.

I took the hit on my shoulder, and the blast of cold was bone cutting as the water soaked my shirt and moved on down, sticking my clothes to me, leaving my chin dripping.

The group divided around me and went on down the hill. One of the guys muttered, "Sorry, babe," as he passed.

Well, at least it was spring and the water didn't feel all that bad. Wanda would have some clothes I could put on. But it made me angry.

The next day, Saturday, was incredibly beautiful—air so soft and warm it drew me out of the house to just walk around, feeling the breeze on my face. Lots of college kids were out, too—milling in front of the frat houses and drifting downtown.

I saw some graffiti on retaining walls and sidewalks about the war. In front of the restaurant where I went to pick up meatball sandwiches for Mary Suzanne's and my supper, a bunch of kids were blocking the sidewalk. A tall guy with an Afro raised his fist in a cry for power to the people.

That night, the sirens alerted us to something going on out by the campus. Mary Suzanne and I went into the front yard and watched an orange glow in the sky. People going by said it was the ROTC building on fire—that students were burning it because they wanted ROTC off campus and an end to the war.

Even after I finally went to bed, the smell of the fire kept me awake for a long time. I thought about home and Megan and what had happened to my friends. I wondered where in Canada Ray was, and how he was doing. At some point, I drifted from a fitful sleep to hear voices from the street chanting, "One, two, three, four. We don't want your fucking war." Cambodia. That was making everything worse.

When I came downstairs Sunday morning, Mary Suzanne's door was still closed. A warm breeze swept through the house. The sun, coming through a redbud tree, threw a peaceful light into the kitchen.

I went out on the porch to get the paper. The street had a morning-after-a-wild-party look. A poster that read BURN THE FUCKER DOWN! and, below that, BLOW THE FUCKER UP! had been abandoned in the yard. Somebody's red T-shirt dangled from a white picket fence that had been partly knocked over. The couch the fraternity boys had dragged out onto their porch roof lay feet-up in the yard like a large dead animal.

But everything was quiet now. A robin picked up some litter from the sidewalk and flew into a tree. It was all over. The National Guard was here and order was restored.

Mr. Delving telephoned while I was getting ready for school Monday morning. "I can get you out of class for a special journalism project if you want to go on campus and report on the peace rally scheduled for noon."

I'd planned to paint scenery for the spring play with Lena and a couple of other friends, but Dad would be so proud that I'd been given an important journalism assignment.

I knocked on the bathroom doors to ask my substitute parent if I could.

Mary Suzanne hesitated. "I guess the Guard will keep everything under control," she eventually said.

Yesterday, kids had hung around with the Guardsmen who'd been called in Saturday night. I'd seen a girl put a daisy in the rifle of one of them, and he'd given her the peace sign.

Mary Suzanne and I walked to campus together. Guardsmen stood along the street in pairs. We passed really close to a couple of them at the stoplight in front of the bookstore, and I looked into the face of one. He caught my eye and nodded.

"They're so young," I whispered to Mary Suzanne. "And kind of cute."

"Take them out of the uniforms and you couldn't tell them from the students."

She went up the hill to Satterfield Hall, and I drifted across the campus, making notes. I wanted to see what was left of the burned ROTC building, but it was still surrounded by dozens of Guardsmen. One, with a stony face, moved in front of me, his legs apart, the butt of his rifle planted on the ground. He didn't look like the sort of person who would welcome a flower in his rifle barrel. "This area is off-limits," he growled.

So I went over to the Student Union. Trying to blend in and look like a college student, I joined a cluster of kids reading the administration announcement on a bulletin board that the noon rally had been canceled.

"They can't do that!" a girl wearing a headband stormed. "It's our campus. We pay tuition. We have a right to gather on the Commons."

"Right on, sister," somebody agreed.

The rally was supposed to be at the Victory Bell, on the Commons between the Union and Taylor Hall. There were a few kids around the Victory Bell when I got there about ten forty-five, but it looked more like a picnic than a peace rally. The grass had turned lush over the weekend, and a couple lay under a magnolia tree sharing a joint, oblivious.

I sat down in the shade to make some notes. On a nearby boulder, someone had spray-painted FUCK YOU, AGNEW. Kids with book bags drifted past. A boy flashed me the peace sign.

The number of students gradually increased as morning classes let out. Some seemed laid-back and curious, but the ones clustered by the Victory Bell looked more determined. A few guys jumped up on it and started leading the chant I'd heard in the streets Friday night. "One, two, three, four. We don't want your fucking war. Five, six, seven, eight . . ."

The bell began to toll, as if calling the students to gather, and I joined the crowd.

I looked over my shoulder, back at the burned ROTC building. Maybe a hundred or two hundred Guardsmen seemed focused on us. Someone was driving around in a jeep with a bullhorn. "This assembly is unlawful. You must disperse immediately. This is an order."

"Off our campus, pigs!" a girl beside me screamed, giving the jeep the finger with both hands, and somebody threw a rock, which fell short of its mark.

The bullhorn kept on with its message. The bell kept ringing, and students kept pouring onto the Commons.

But good journalists are exact. How many? I couldn't tell. Hundreds. I looked up the hill and around Taylor Hall and Prentice Hall and the Student Union. Maybe five hundred. And the tolling bell seemed to be bringing even more.

I looked at my watch. Almost noon. Time for the rally to start.

I smelled perfume and pot and body odor. Some of the faces were just curious, but others were tense and angry. Surely the Guard could keep the peace. But their presence seemed to make the students angrier.

"Get off our campus, motherfuckers!" somebody screamed back at the Guardsmen.

I heard a *thunking* sound, and something arched high through the air—something silver that caught the sunlight. A whole bunch of Guardsmen began to move toward us.

"Tear gas! Bastards! They're shooting tear gas at us!"

A boy ripped off his shirt, picked up a canister, ran straight back toward the troops, and tossed it into their midst. Other kids screamed encouragement.

As the Guard got closer, a guy darted from behind a tree. A girl grabbed for him, seeming to try to pull him back. A gold peace-sign earring dangled from her ear.

The boy flung a handful of rocks at a Guardsman, who whirled and slashed at him with a baton. I heard the cracking noise and fled. But somebody had dropped a book bag in the surge, and I tripped over it, falling, twisting my ankle. The girl with the peace-sign earring grabbed my hand and helped me up.

Running away in the confusion was hard because there were hundreds of kids and at least a hundred Guardsmen going first this way and then that way. And I couldn't tell where *away* was.

The bell kept tolling and the tear gas kept spewing and the kids kept screaming, "Kill the motherfucking pigs!"

I limped, moving as fast as I could, weaving among the crowd, looking for clear space. Somebody grabbed my shirt and I yanked away. This was crazy!

"Kill the pigs, kill the pigs, kill the pigs." The chant was coming from the left, so I tried to work my way right, going past the pagoda.

But the Guardsmen, looking like aliens with their gas masks, seemed to be trying to herd us. One of them shoved me aside and I heard a series of *thunking* noises. The breeze caught the tear gas and carried it toward the chanters, who made obscene gestures and stood their ground as long as they could—when the gas reached them, though, they fled with their shirts lifted over their faces.

My ankle was killing me, but there was no place to stop. No way out. Kids had found a pile of construction debris that they were flinging at the Guard—big pieces of what looked like concrete. And boards with nails in them.

About fifty Guardsmen knelt, taking some kind of funny position. What were they doing?

I screamed, scrambled backward, coming out of the

worst of the melee into a parking lot. I was upwind from the tear gas, but its burning odor still hung in the air and stung my throat.

At last the crowd seemed to flow into the parking lot and lose momentum, like a breaking wave on the beach. The Guardsmen who had been kneeling stood up and re-formed into smaller groups. They started back toward the pagoda.

We were drifting apart. Thank God, it was ending.

Students began to straggle away, looking back at the Guardsmen. One kid made a violent gesture as he turned, jumping up and down in rage. Stupid kid. Somebody could have really gotten hurt.

I looked at my watch. Twelve twenty-three.

I bent down to rub my ankle. When I stood up, I saw a small group of Guardsmen back by the pagoda turn together, raise their rifles as if on command, and begin firing straight at us.

People screamed.

Someone roared, "Cease firing, cease firing, cease firing!" But the guns kept on making their cracking noises, and the ejected cartridges clanged as they fell.

I threw myself down, my bare arms hitting the concrete, the grit mashing itself into my cheeks. I put my hands over my head, praying I wouldn't get shot or trampled. Feet pounded around me. "Oh God, Dad," I kept saying over and over through clenched teeth. "Oh God, Dad."

Then the shooting seemed to stop. But I didn't move or open my eyes. Kids were screaming. People were whimpering. Somebody groaned. Guard officers barked out commands. I smelled a hot, sweet, coppery smell.

When I felt footsteps near me and heard the sirens starting in the distance, I raised myself up, shaking so hard I couldn't even brush away the hair that was stuck to my face.

The girl with the peace-sign earring lay on her side a few feet away. A Guardsman knelt beside her. Bright red blood ran down her neck and turned her blouse dark.

I half crawled and half slid toward her. The Guardsman turned on me, snarling, "Keep away! Clear the area!" His face was contorted. He bellowed, "Everybody clear the area!"

I shied back until my butt came up against a curb, then I sat waiting. The Guardsman had bowed his head over the girl and was chanting, "Medic, medic, medic." His eyes were shut and he was holding the girl's hand. "Oh, girl, don't die. Don't die."

"Disperse!" A Guardsman was roaming around yelling at students. "Clear the area!"

The smell of tear gas still hung in the air. Students fled in all directions. It seemed so quiet after the gunfire, despite all the yelling.

A police car came rocking across the grass of the Commons, siren sounding. Two ambulances screamed into the parking lot. When I saw medics with a stretcher running toward the girl, I stood up and began backing away. As they squatted beside her, I turned and ran the best I could with my hurt ankle back toward Main Street.

I thought I heard somebody shouting my name, but I looked around and didn't see anybody I knew.

"Jill!" I looked back again and saw John running toward me. "Are you hurt?" he asked, breathless. "You're bleeding."

"My ankle hurts. I fell."

"Well, your head is bleeding." He lifted back my matted hair.

"Were you there?" I asked.

He nodded, his eyes looking like he wasn't awake yet from the worst imaginable nightmare. His shirt was ripped on one shoulder and his face was smudged. His clothing carried the smell of tear gas.

"I think you're just skinned," he said, touching my forehead.

"Is it over?" I asked, quaking inside. If it could happen once, who was to say it couldn't go on happening? "A girl right by me was shot."

"A lot of people were shot. But I think it's over." His voice was quavering.

"Why did they shoot at us?" I cried, breaking down. I was Jill Snow, a sixteen-year-old high school girl from Jefferson, Iowa. My dad was Jim Snow, a newspaper publisher.

Nobody was supposed to shoot at me! The sense of astonishment was so great I dropped to my knees and began pounding on the grass. How could people shoot at me?

"Jill, baby. Jill, baby." John was rubbing my back. "Take a deep breath. It's all over."

He got me to my feet and held me tight as we walked. At first we were among other students like ourselves, all of us in shock. But as we went farther west on Main Street toward Mary Suzanne's apartment, the crowd thinned out.

A police car cruised slowly down the street, using the bull horn. "Firestone, close up." It rolled down the street a little farther. "Union Seventy-six, close up." A little farther. "You boys get back in your fraternity houses and stay there." When it was abreast of us, the cop rolled down his window.

"Where are you two going?"

"That house there," John said, still supporting me. "She lives there. With her sister. A professor at the college."

"We're closing the college," he said. "Closing the town. We're under martial law now." Then, more kindly, he asked if I needed medical attention.

I shook my head no, putting my hand over my face.

Mary Suzanne kept dabbing my head with hydrogen peroxide. I don't think she realized what she was doing.

I pushed her hand away. "Stop."

This would be all over the news and Dad would be worried sick. We couldn't get through to him, though—the phone lines were overloaded and produced only a perpetual busy signal.

The chop of a helicopter came so close it sounded as if it were landing on our roof. Mary Suzanne put her hands over her ears. "What have they done to my college?" she kept saying. "What have they done to my college? I can't even go to my office. My notes are there. My research. Students' papers. How will I give grades?"

"Mary Suzanne, kids are dead."

She looked at me. She shook her head. She didn't get it yet.

We kept trying to call Dad and still got the same busy signal. We stayed glued to the television. They talked incessantly about whether a command to fire was given, but all I remembered was someone yelling, "Cease firing, cease firing, cease firing." I thought of the line in a Yeats poem Mr. Steig had assigned: "The falcon cannot hear the falconer; things fall apart; the center cannot hold."

About midnight, when I'd just begun to drift off to sleep, the phone rang. I heard Mary Suzanne's voice downstairs and knew Dad had finally gotten through. She tried to keep her voice low, but I heard parts of what she said, telling Dad I'd been in the middle of it, that a girl right by me had been shot, that I'd hurt my ankle and scraped my face, that I was asleep.

I knew my sister felt guilty. She was supposed to be keeping me safe. "Her journalism teacher asked her to go," she was explaining, her voice getting louder. "We thought the trouble was all over, Dad. We thought with the Guard there the campus was perfectly safe."

She listened for a while, then I heard her say, "Oh, Dad, you shouldn't feel guilty either. Nobody could possibly have imagined . . ."

Eventually, she came up the stairs and stood silently in the doorway.

"I'm awake," I admitted.

"You want to talk to Dad?"

I hobbled downstairs and sat on the couch in the dark living room. "Dad?"

"Jill."

I started bawling, great sobbing gasps, over the steady thrum of his comforting voice. He didn't tell me everything would be okay, but he told me he loved me, he would do anything for me, he would come and get me, he wanted me home, he would be here as soon as he could get on a plane.

Finally, Mary Suzanne gave me a wad of tissues and took the telephone. After she said good-bye to Dad, we sat on the couch in the darkness. A helicopter hovered nearby, its blades beating the air, and a searchlight swung briefly over us before it lifted off.

The honeysuckle outside the window sweetened the breeze. The town was dark and quiet as we kept the curfew of martial law.

Jill and I carried my stuff downstairs, and Dad packed it into the VW. I made a last check of the room to make sure I hadn't forgotten anything. I looked out the dormer window at Main Street. The couch still lay belly up in the Delta Tau Delta yard.

"I'll bet you'll be glad to have your study back," I told Jill, then regretted my words. She no longer had any football player students to help her move her desk.

She sighed, reading my mind. "It's okay."

"Are you going to be all right here by yourself?"

"Tom's going to come and spend some time," she said.

I gave her a hug.

As Dad and I drove west, I thought about what going home meant. Mom would be pretty much like she always was, and I tried not to have any hope or expectation of changing that.

Dad didn't have much to say, but taking care of me seemed to please him. He asked me constantly if I was hungry or thirsty or needed to go to the bathroom and bought me treats every time we stopped for gas.

Whatever awful thing had come between us seemed to have disappeared. I was hardly even aware of the space it left.

Megan would want to know everything about that day, but I wouldn't be able to tell her. I wouldn't be able to tell anybody ever.

I'd gotten some letters from Crissy and had answered her. I ached to hug her. Megan said she was her same old silly self, but thin and scarred from the surgeries.

Maybe we could go out to Spring Lake and build a beach fire and listen to music and smoke a little pot. I'd smoked pot now and then at John and Wanda's place, but it wasn't the same as doing it with old friends.

I leaned back, my eyes half-shut, feeling the air from the vent brush my legs. Dad's profile, against the south sun, made him look reliable and everlasting, like the head on a coin.

When we crossed the Mississippi River, I sat up and said *Hello, Iowa*, to myself.

Just after we left Iowa City, Dad began to talk about his boyhood. This time it wasn't about things like unpaved roads and the horrors of the Depression. He talked about family who'd died before I was born and people like Aunt Cathy, who I'd never really gotten a chance to know. About his brother Amos and his mom and dad and how hard it was to be a parent. About his best friend, Noah. About his first wife, Julia, and Julia's brother, who'd been killed during the Second World War. He told me how much he'd hated to go into the army, though he wanted to serve his country, but he didn't want to leave his young wife and Mary Suzanne and his little sister, Cathy, who'd been only sixteen—my age.

"I always tried to look out for Cathy," Dad said, and I heard his voice break. "Just like I always tried to look out for you and Mary Suzanne."

I saw a tear run down his cheek and reached over to brush it away. I didn't want him to cry, though I was crying myself.

"You can't take care of all the little girls, Dad," I said, which really seemed kind of funny, and I found myself laughing.

Dad glanced at me. Then he began to laugh, too, and took my hand and held it tight.

Mona
2006

Chapter One

WHILE I WAITED to pay for the milk and oranges, I browsed a copy of the *Trib*. A front-page story about Afghanistan had Mom's byline: *Jill Snow*. I rubbed my little gold pendant like I always did when I saw her byline and she wasn't home yet. The U.S. Embassy bombing in Tanzania, the U.S.S. *Cole*, the London train and bus bombings—Mom had covered all of them. The pendant was worn almost smooth.

Outside, the Chicago heat squeezed me so hard I could barely breathe. An idling produce truck stunk up the air. When I was crossing the street to our apartment building, my cell phone rang. I checked caller ID and felt the usual euphoria that Mom had not been blown to bits by a suicide bomber or run over by a tank. "Where are you?" I asked.

"At O'Hare waiting for the train. Where are you?"

"Just getting home. I saw your story."

A jet engine screamed in the background. "I can't hear you," Mom said. "I'll be there in an hour."

Inside our apartment, I put the food away and peeled an orange, leaving the skin on the counter so it made the stuffy, unused kitchen smell better. Then I checked e-mail.

Stanza wrote, "Guess what? Aunt Con has invited my cousin Robi and me to sail the Greek Isles with her for a month. Robi is bringing a friend, and so can I. How about you????????????? We leave on Wednesday."

Please let Mom say yes. Who wanted to hang around here by myself all summer?

Stanza went on to tell me how much fun living in New York was, but how lonely, too, and she really hoped I could come on the trip with her family.

I heard Mom's key in the lock.

"Baby?" she called, coming down the hall. As she hugged me, I felt her warmth through her silk jacket and caught the deep smell of some perfume that seemed to be always on her, though I'd never actually seen her dab any on. Was it like pheromones—something girls naturally smelled on their mothers?

"Follow me while I get out of these clothes," she said, starting toward the master bedroom at the other end of the apartment. Then she turned, hugging me again, giving me a smacking kiss on the cheek. "It's so good to see you. Were you this tall four days ago? I hate leaving you. I've told my editors I'm absolutely not taking any more of these out-of-the-country assignments."

"You always say that."

She slipped out of her skirt. "Did your father think you were tall and beautiful?"

I shrugged. Lunch with my father had been a sort of cosmic nonevent. But then, I'd seen him about ten times in my whole life.

"Why'd you marry him?" I asked.

She tied up her frizzy blond hair and stepped into her shower. "I actually *married* your dad in a fit of misguided political conformity." She tilted her face back and just stood there for a while, letting the water course down her body. "I thought one day it might matter to you that you had divorced parents like everybody else." She laughed.

"That's not funny, Mom. I want the truth. I'm sixteen."

She turned the water off and pulled a towel around herself, looking at me. I hoped I hadn't pissed her off. I wanted her to say yes to the sailing.

She began, "Once my mother asked me if I was happy being sixteen." She brushed her hair, looking in the mirror and not at me. "It was one of the few times in my teens she *really* noticed me."

My grandmother had died the year I was born. "Wasn't she a good mother?"

"She was stuck in the middle of nowhere with nothing to do. She was depressed before antidepressants." Mom looked at me. "I did not give her joy." She spaced the words bluntly.

I almost shivered, despite the steamy heat.

"So I decided that my child, if I was ever lucky enough to have one, would be the most important thing in the world to me. But then I got busy with work and my biological clock was on its last tick. So I married the nicest, brightest, best-looking guy in the correspondents' pool—your dad. When I found out I was pregnant, I promised the gods that I would never, *ever* not pay attention to you."

Tears came to my eyes. So much love weighted me down sometimes. Crowded me. And I wanted to sail with Stanza.

Mom stepped back. "I'll make some tea."

Her hot green tea laced with honey tasted like ambrosia.

As we sat across from each other at the kitchen island, I told her about Stanza's aunt and the sailing trip.

"I really want to go. I'd only be away a few weeks," I said, curling my legs around the stool in tense hope. "So how about it?"

"But you'd have to travel all that way by yourself."

"Didn't I take my first steps down the aisle of a Boeing?" I asked, trying to make her laugh.

When I was little, Mom dragged me around the world in the care of a nanny. But once I started school, I'd stayed pretty much in Chicago.

She gave me a look. "They say summer travel will be horrible. Security issues, overbooking, delays. You'd probably spend the whole month at Heathrow."

Which would beat spending it in Chicago. She watched my face.

"Come on, sweetie," she finally said. "For the first time, in ages, I'm planning to be *here* most of the summer."

I held the hot, thin edge of the china cup to my lips, looking away. How many summers—and winters, springs, and falls—had I waited with a housekeeper or a nanny for *her* to come back from somewhere?

She gave a deep, long, martyred-mother sigh. "Okay."

I felt so guilty I almost agreed to stay home after all. But instead I went over and rested my cheek in the nest of her hair. "Thanks, Mom."

The phone rang.

"It's Grandpa," she said, glancing at the caller ID.

She listened and then met my eyes. She scribbled a note, which she pushed over to me. "Aunt Cathy died."

Chapter Two

AUNT CATHY HAD wanted her funeral in Savannah where she'd lived, but she'd left instructions that her ashes were to be brought back to Jefferson, Iowa. "Dad wants us to come," Mom said. "She was his little sister, and this is hard on him."

So Wednesday, the day I should have been stepping aboard a sailboat, Mom and I were driving to Iowa. The afternoon sun gave me a horrible headache. I kicked off my Crocs, shut my eyes, and pretended to be listening to my iPod. What good would I do anybody in Iowa? I barely knew my great-aunt or the people we'd be seeing.

When we crossed the river at Davenport, Mom poked my leg. "Look at the Mississippi, Mona. There's something about this river. Of all the rivers I've crossed, this one's the most important."

Why this should be the most important river to my mother I didn't know. I only knew there was nothing to

Iowa but rolling hills of crops and that it took forever to get to the little town where Grandpa Jim lived.

At dusk, we parked in front of the old Lincoln Hotel in Jefferson. There was nobody around, so when I got out of the car I pulled my shorts away from my sweaty rear end and bent down, touching my toes and stretching.

Everything in the lobby of the old hotel was closed and empty. We walked up the broad, open flight of wooden stairs and passed the stained-glass window of stylized corn on the landing. Mom pushed the buzzer on Grandpa Jim's door.

My grandfather was ninety. The last time I'd seen him, he'd still lived in the big house where Mom and her sister had grown up. This was going to be so depressing.

When he opened the door, he looked taller than I remembered, thin, and still handsome. Suspenders held up his khakis. He had on a long-sleeved blue shirt and a red bowtie. He hugged Mom, then me—standing back, gripping my arms, looking at me.

"Hi, Grandpa Jim."

His expression was so interested. "Hi, Mona Snow."

The way he said it made me laugh and glance at Mom.

Then he turned to lead us through a small entryway. "Come in, come in."

Stanza had dragged me along once to visit an elderly relative who lived in two rooms crammed with ancestral carved furniture that had reeked of lavender bath powder. So I didn't know what to say as a wide-open, sparsely furnished space opened out in front of Grandpa Jim. He had knocked out walls, I guessed. Two sides were floor-to-ceiling windows, and the wooden floor glowed in the low sun. Shelves of books, like a library, stood two deep around the edges.

"I didn't know you had a loft!"

A domed skylight arched over a large desk in the middle of the room.

"Is that what I've got?" His glasses glinted in the light.

"And you brought all your books from the old house."

"I just found this to show you," he said, taking a faded volume from a stack. "It was my mother's favorite."

The Magnificent Ambersons. I opened it. "Mona Snow, 1918" was written inside the cover. So that's why he'd greeted me by my full name.

He went to find the tea makings for Mom.

And what was I supposed to do?

I picked up another old book embossed with gold. It fell open to a poem titled "The Night-Piece: To Julia" about a girl who was what Stanza would call a *hottie*. Hadn't my grandfather once been married to a woman named Julia?

I wandered around and found a framed copy of Mom's story about the Kent State shootings, which had been published in the Jefferson *Herald*. The ink of her autograph had turned a weird purple. "To Dad with love from Jill—my first big story."

"We're back, Uncle Jim." Two boys banged in with grocery bags. The one about my age looked startled when he saw me. "Whoa."

Whoa? I looked like a horse?

"Hey, you remember me? I'm David." He took off his baseball cap. His forehead had a band of white where his tan ended. And he wore a sweaty red T-shirt with a yellow tornado on the front. "I pushed you out of our hayloft when we were eight."

Could these guys be my cousins?

"These are Amos's grandsons," Grandpa Jim said. "You remember Chris and David."

Chris put down the groceries and shook hands with Mom. "We sometimes read your stuff in my political science class at Iowa State," he said. "I tell them you're from Jefferson, Iowa, but I don't think they believe me."

The boys put away Grandpa Jim's groceries. Chris couldn't quite let go of how proud he was to be related to Mom, the famous political correspondent.

David juggled three oranges, grinning at me. Then he slid them into the fridge. "Hey, tomorrow night, after all of the family stuff, maybe you'd like to ride around. I could introduce you to some kids. Show you our cabin out on the Raccoon River."

The Raccoon River was hardly the Aegean. But I was here and it was there, and it might give me something to tell Stanza about.

Mom turned into the little cemetery lane where a few wild daisies grew out of the gravel. We were several cars back from the limousines that Great-aunt Cathy's family was getting out of. Grandpa Jim emerged, and a girl my age—Great-aunt Cathy's great-granddaughter, Zoey—took his arm. People were drifting toward the green awning, the scene unreal because of the silence. A bird blurted out a long, pretty song so startling my heart beat faster for a second.

Mom and I walked single file along the line of cars leading to the gravesite. I tried to stay on the gravel, brushing against the cars, which were hot in the sun. Was it okay to walk in the grass that people were buried under? I wished Mom were walking in front of me.

As we got closer, I heard Great-aunt Cathy's family talking to each other in their soft southern voices. People drifted among the graves. Chris and David, their faces solemn, were with Uncle Amos's clan. A clump of about twenty people who looked as if they could all belong to Aunt Mary Suzanne in one way or another stood near her, and she held the hand of a little girl with reddish gold braids who called her Nana.

Under the awning, a few rows of chairs faced a stand draped with a white cloth. A bouquet of pink roses stood beside it. An Episcopal priest marked something in a book, then strolled off to talk to Grandpa Jim and Great-aunt Cathy's family.

I took Mom's hand. How odd we must look, just the two of us. The other families milled in herds, protected by men wearing wedding rings and dress shirts.

Actually, Mom and I belonged to Grandpa Jim, but he was being claimed by Great-aunt Cathy's people.

Somebody had laid a wreath of fresh flowers over my great-grandparents' grave. *WILLIAM SNOW, 1886–1950,* and *MONA SNOW, 1888–1952.*

I walked on, finding the graves of Great-uncle Amos and his wife, and a young daughter named Elizabeth.

"She died of polio," Mom murmured. "And their son, Max, was killed in Nam." She pointed to another grave. "And here's my mother's grave."

"Is it time to start, Uncle Jim?" a man asked my grandfather.

"Yes—" He broke off, looking toward the road. "Wait."

Everybody turned to watch two people making their way toward us.

"I think that's Mary Ann Miller. She and Cathy were great friends when they were girls," he explained. His voice went reedy and his face was wrecked with sudden grief.

I told myself not to cry, because then I would sniffle and my face would itch and it wouldn't make my grandfather feel any better. My feet and ankles already itched from the grass seed I'd picked up in my sandals.

When the elderly woman, deeply shaded in a sun hat, finally reached us, she turned loose of the arm of the young man supporting her and clasped my grandfather's hand. Grandpa Jim escorted her to the awning and they sat down. There weren't nearly enough chairs for everybody, and they were all taken by Great-aunt Cathy's family, except for an empty one beside my grandfather.

The priest opened his book. We were still. I saw a tiny ant crawling over the top of my foot and willed myself not to move.

My grandfather beckoned to Aunt Mary Suzanne and touched the empty seat at his side. She turned loose of her little granddaughter's hand and went to sit beside him.

The service was short and not very sad, really. A closing. Still, my throat ached and I found myself rubbing the little gold pendant through the linen of my sundress until I made the fabric shiny. I swallowed, wondering if it sounded as loud to anybody else as it did to me.

David and Chris's dad invited everybody out to their place for a meal. Mom began hugging and talking to people. I just stood there by myself. People were gathered around Grandpa Jim, and then like in a crowded room when everybody stops talking at once, he was just standing there by himself, too.

When I went over to him, he seemed composed. Relieved. He put his hand on my shoulder, and I could feel him trembling a little. "How are you doing with this big family?" he asked, his voice raspy.

"Okay." I tried to smile. "Kind of . . . lonely, maybe."

A little line of whiskers he'd missed shaving glinted silver in the sunshine. He nodded. "So many Snows. Living and dead."

"Where is your first wife buried?" I asked. "Julia."

He took my hand. "Right over here. I'll show you."

The Goodwins were only a few graves away. Grandpa Jim rested his hand on my shoulder as we stood reading the headstones. Millicent and Art Goodwin. Paul Goodwin. Julia Goodwin Snow.

I hoped I hadn't made my grandfather sadder by asking.

"A nice thing about being old, Mona," he said, as if reading my mind, "is you have so many memories."

A long-stemmed pink rose lay on top of Paul Goodwin's headstone.

"Look," I said, pointing. "That's from Great-aunt Cathy's bouquet."

Grandpa Jim looked at the rose for a long time. "Maybe

Mary Ann put it there," he finally said. "She and Cathy were sixteen together, and they had their secrets." He cleared his throat. "I was sixteen when I fell in love with Julia."

Well, I was sixteen, and no love in sight.

The sun was beating down. My grandfather should be in the shade. I took his arm and led him toward the big tree that sheltered the Snows.

Chapter Three

THE SUN WAS almost down, the sky turquoise. Large clouds on the horizon that could be thunderheads were backlit by pink.

My hair frizzed in the wind of the open jeep. We headed down a gravel road, going fast. I turned to look at the fantail of dust behind.

David pointed to the left. "I baled that hay yesterday," he yelled over his shoulder. Fat, golden rolls threw long shadows over the field.

David's girlfriend, Coral, reached into a cooler, opened four bottles of beer, and passed them around. After a while, we cut down a private lane—hilly, curvy, and rough—toward the Raccoon River. David tooted the horn as we passed a little silver trailer at the edge of the woods. In the deep twilight, a boy was loading huge cans of something into an old pickup.

David braked. "Come down," he called.

The boy made a salute of acknowledgment and hefted two more big cans into the back of the truck.

"Who's that?" I asked.

"Adam Ludgate. He and his dad caretake the place."

The large cabin was on a bluff, with decks on different levels stepping down to the river.

"Ah need t' pee," Zoey said—the *ah* making it sound elegant and ladylike.

David pushed open the cabin door, flipped a switch that turned on some lamps, and said, "Straight through, on your right."

We ended up sitting around the table, having another beer, playing dominos, and listening to a Shania Twain album while demented June bugs bashed against the screens.

After a while, we left off the dominos and just talked about the day, explaining things to Coral. "What did you think when Uncle Jim asked Mary Suzanne to come and sit with us?" Zoey asked.

David rolled his eyes.

I remembered how it had made my mother smile. "Why did he do that?"

Zoey looked at me. "You mean y'all don't *know*?"

I shook my head.

"Well, see . . ." David began, then he got started laughing.

Coral picked up his almost-empty bottle and drank the rest herself. "No more for you, boy-o," she said.

Zoey laid her hand on my arm. "Mind you, hon, my great-grandmother was very much a southern lady. I only knew her as the family matriarch in her great white pillared house taking tea with the rector, but when she was our age . . ." She wiggled her brows. "Ooh la la!"

"Cathy was Mary Suzanne's real mother," David said bluntly. "That's why Mary Suzanne sat with the family."

I blinked. Aunt Mary Suzanne was Mom's half-sister. "No. She's Grandpa Jim's daughter."

"He found her under a cabbage leaf," David said.

"She was adopted by Uncle Jim and his first wife, Julia," Zoey explained, giving him a look. "But she was really the love child of sixteen-year-old Cathy and a young soldier."

I just sat there. Until yesterday, my family had seemed to have so little to do with me. Now I found out people weren't even who I thought they were.

I remembered the pink rose on the Goodwin boy's headstone. "Julia's brother was the father of Cathy's baby," I said.

David threw up his arms. "Touchdown!"

I glared at him. Maybe I just hadn't had enough beer, but I didn't like feeling stupid—not about my own family, not about important stuff that everybody else seemed to know. "I think I'll go down to the dock for a while," I said, standing up.

❧

I sat on the end of the dock for what seemed like a long time. I wanted to go home. Wherever that was.

Thunder rumbled distantly and lightning bounced around in the clouds. Now and then I could make out music and voices from the house. And I heard car doors slamming.

I thought it was David until he spoke. "Sky's pretty all lit up, innit?" He had a soft, slow way of talking.

"Yes." Could he tell by my voice I'd been crying?

He sat down beside me on the end of the dock. "I'm Adam."

The sky lit up with fine crazed lines, like a web.

"I'm Mona. David's cousin."

We sat there. A bullfrog sang from the rushes, and then one called from the opposite bank. Something leaped in the water.

"I like watching storms come in," he said.

"Is this where you watch from?"

"Yeah."

The breeze ruffled the smell of something sweet. "Wild honeysuckle," he said. "Over there." When he pointed, his arm brushed mine. "I'm sorry to hear about your relative dyin'."

"Oh, she was my great-aunt who I'd not seen in years." I kept my voice soft, not wanting to disturb the river life.

"Still," he said.

"Still," I echoed. "What were you putting in the truck when we came by? It looked heavy."

"Paint. Dad and I paint metal farm buildings. Come up from Chattanooga every summer. It's how we earn college money for my brother and me. My brother's in veterinary school now. I'm next. This caretaking job with a place to stay is just gravy." Pause. "What are you doin' down here by yourself? The party's up there."

"Just thinking." About the book with my name in it going back almost a hundred years. Julia in her silky clothes. Aunt Cathy hooked up with a soldier and having a baby at sixteen.

Adam lay back on the dock and cupped his hands beneath his head. He was quiet for so long that I wondered if he'd fallen asleep. The river made a shushing, trickling sound.

"Hey." I jumped when Adam spoke. "Lay back," he said. "Lay back and look straight up. When it lightnings, you can see amazing things in the depths of the sky."

The boards felt uncomfortable against my shoulder blades at first, and it was hard for me to really look. But as the light played through the clouds, I began to pick out hidden depths to the sky, surprising cloud formations, layer on layer of complications.

"I've never seen the sky this way," I said, after a while. I was losing my orientation, feeling a little sleepy.

"Just keep looking." His voice sounded far away.

The changing air sent cool little fingers tickling over my body. A wind rushed toward us, rattling the leaves first, stirring the river, then finally catching my hair. Several drops of rain fell quickly, making bursts of cold against my stretched-out body.

Adam jumped up and held out his hand. I was dizzy when I stood up and clutched the front of his T-shirt. His body was solid and nice when I leaned against him.

"Careful," he whispered, "you don't want to fall in the river."

I shook my head, and there was a moment when I didn't breathe and I don't think he did either.

"Come on," he said, his voice low. "It's raining." He held my arm as we ran for the cabin.

The rain stopped as suddenly as it had started, though thunder still popped all around. Chris was outside the cabin talking to David, and I saw some other kids inside. The music was louder and Chris was saying, "You get your license, Dad buys you a car, and you drink beer while you're driving?"

"Jeez, sorry, dude."

"I'll take Mona home," Adam said, interrupting. "I don't think she's in a party mood."

Chris looked at me, eyebrows raised.

I nodded.

"I'll babysit this bunch," Chris said, going in the cabin. David made a sad-clown face and followed him.

"Truck's a mess," Adam said, leading me into the darkness, opening the door, brushing something off the seat, and helping me in.

The truck smelled of paint and turpentine, but when we got back on the gravel road, the night air blew through the cabin. The sky still shimmered now and then with light.

Crissy's husband was in the den watching TV when I got there. He muted his hockey game long enough to say, "The girls are upstairs. Back in the bedroom."

The girls? It made them sound like Stanza and me, holed up in her room, replaying a date. What would Stanza say if she knew I'd met a slow-talking boy from Chattanooga who'd almost kissed me in a thunderstorm?

I walked down the upstairs corridor toward the sound of my mom's laughter. What was that smell?

Mom, seeing me, pointed to her hair, which had weird blue snakelike streaks in it. "Whadda you think?"

Crissy held a little white brush, meeting my look of alarm in the mirror. "Don't worry, sweetie. The blue is just the color of the goop so you can see where ya' been. Your mom will have pretty highlights when we're done. We used to do this when we were kids."

I sat on the edge of the bed, which had picture albums and scrapbooks spread all over. I could spot Mom and Crissy and people I couldn't name but who kept appearing in picture after picture.

There Mom was at her sixteenth birthday party, standing by a VW. Grandpa Jim looked so *young*.

Crissy and Mom came to look over my shoulder. "Remember what we used to do in that car?" Crissy said.

"The world was safe then," Mom murmured. She sighed. "I feel so safe *here*, don't you, Mona?" she asked, trailing her fingers through my hair.

I yanked away. How could she settle back into her old life as if she'd never left Jefferson?

"Actually, I feel very bored here." I made my voice cold, knowing it wasn't even true.

Mom shot me a look and glanced at her old friend.

"Well!" Crissy said, trilling the word, trying to laugh it off.

Mom looked so hurt. I turned a page of one of the albums, letting out my breath. There was a snapshot of Mom and Aunt Mary Suzanne in bathing suits sitting around somebody's swimming pool.

"Mom, why didn't you ever tell me about Aunt Cathy and the soldier? About Aunt Mary Suzanne?"

Mom looked into her glass. "Where'd you hear about that?"

"*All* my cousins know."

Her eyes snapped to mine. "I'm *sorry*! Everybody's known about it for a long time. I guess I assumed you knew, too."

"Well, how would I know if you didn't tell me?" I demanded, hearing my voice break. "I'm not from around here like you are, where you just suck up information from the stratosphere. Look at all these pictures."

I grabbed one of the oldest albums. "Look!" I pointed at one of Mom hanging upside down on a swing set behind the old house where she and Mary Suzanne grew up. Grandpa Jim was measuring the distance from the ground to the tip of one of Mom's ponytails that dangled on either side of her head.

"Look!" I pointed to one in a later album. Mom and Crissy were in the back yard of the old house, eating ice cream cones and doing a kind of silly cheesecake pose.

"Look, look, look, and look!" I blew through the albums pointing to pictures of her. "Don't you notice that nothing changes in these pictures except that you and your friends get older? You're in the same bedroom, the same house, the same town, the same school, the same park. No wonder you feel so damned *safe* here!"

"Mona!" Tears sprung to Mom's eyes.

"Most kids would give their Sunday socks to have the kind of life you've had, kiddo," Crissy said, her voice indignant.

What did Mom's old friend, who probably hadn't lived anywhere but Jefferson since the day she was born, know about my life?

"Sometimes Mom drags me around like I'm a purse," I told her. "I'm going to sleep at Grandpa Jim's tonight," I snapped back. "Leave me alone!"

I kinda knew where Grandpa Jim lived. I mean, Jefferson wasn't Chicago. But how did I get there exactly? The rain was pounding on the sidewalk.

"Hey."

There was the muddy truck and Adam, still parked where he had been a few minutes ago. "Don't you have anything better to do?" I demanded, sorry he was seeing me with tears and snot all over my face.

He leaned across the seat and opened the door. "Nope."

Chapter Four

I HADN'T BEEN able to barge in on my grandfather after midnight. So after Adam and I drove around for a while, I called Mom and told her I was coming back to Crissy's house. I intended my cold, flat tone to communicate that I was still really pissed. Her clipped *okay* said that was just fine because she was, too.

The next morning, while Mom was still snoring in the twin bed next to me in Crissy's guest room, I showered, scribbled a note, and let myself out the front.

As I stood at Grandpa Jim's door, the smell of something rich and grainy floated in the hallway. He had circles under his eyes, but he smiled when he saw me. "Mona Snow."

We had a breakfast of oatmeal with lots of sugar, while sitting at the windows, looking down on the square at the statue of Abraham Lincoln that sparkled in the sunshine.

"It rained last night," he said. "So everything looks clean."

I thought about last night. And today. Spending six hours in the car with Mom on the way back to Chicago was going to be gruesome.

"This oatmeal is really good," I said.

"I've eaten it most mornings of my life. And that's a lot of mornings."

"Only about thirty-three thousand," I said, doing some quick mental math.

"That many?" He smiled. "I used to cook it for my little sister, Cathy. And for Mary Suzanne. And for your mom."

"And now me." I felt honored.

After breakfast, I helped Grandpa Jim put the dishes in the dishwasher and told him a little about my friend, Stanza, and how she'd invited me to go sailing.

About eleven, while he was explaining his book-cataloguing project, Mom turned up. She hadn't forgotten our fight. "*A purse!*" she muttered under her breath when I opened the door, then she blew past me and started talking to Grandpa Jim as if I didn't exist.

I'd been having a good time with my grandfather.

I crossed my arms and went over to stare out the window, ignoring them. Then, embarrassed at acting like a brat, I turned around.

Grandpa Jim was looking at me while Mom was blathering on about Ethiopia or something. I rolled my eyes and he gave a small shrug. I think he was tuned in to Mom and me.

Finally, she stood up, saying it was time to go, and Grandpa Jim made his move.

"You know, I hate to spring this on you two," he said. "But I really do need help cataloguing those books."

Mom frowned—probably thinking she had to be back in the office in the morning.

"Here's what I thought," he said, looking at me. "Maybe Mona could stay around for a few days and help. If she wants to." He switched his gaze back to Mom. "If you could spare her."

Stay here?

"I could show her around Jefferson. Of course, that would take all of fifteen minutes," he said, turning his smile to me. "And I could send you home on the bus when you got bored."

When I said "I'd like that," Mom looked at me as if I'd gone crazy. Hadn't I just called the place boring in front of her old friend last night?

"Are you sure, Mona?" she asked.

"I'm sure."

So Mom went back to Chicago and I stayed in Jefferson and slept in Grandpa Jim's tiny guest room.

Grandpa Jim gave me a tour of Jefferson, and it took a

lot more than fifteen minutes. We went by the house where he, Uncle Amos, and Aunt Cathy had been born, which looked a little shabby but was still standing. He showed me the Goodwins' old house, where Julia had lived when he'd dated her. We went by the office of the newspaper he'd edited and published for his whole working life except during part of World War II, and he took me in and introduced me around. I was glad he just said I was his granddaughter, Mona, and didn't mention that I was the daughter of the well-known political correspondent Jill Snow. I could tell by the deference of the people in the office how much they respected my grandfather.

He also told me a lot about our family as I helped him catalogue his books. He described the wide, shallow Platte River, where he and his little sister, Cathy, had waded with the sandhill cranes. "It was the Great Depression," he said. "It's lucky we made it home." About the fighting on Leyte, where he'd been shot in the leg. About his friend Noah, who'd been killed.

Aunt Mary Suzanne came over from Ames to visit us, and Chris and David popped in and out of Grandpa Jim's apartment, doing errands and delivering groceries. And I saw them out at the river sometimes, too.

Turned out the cabin and land along the Raccoon didn't belong to David's and Chris's dad, like I'd assumed. It belonged to the family corporation of G&S Seeds, of which

Mom and I were shareholders. So it was kind of mine. And kind of Zoey's, whom I'd e-mailed a time or two. I finally worked up the nerve to ask if her great-grandmother had been shamed by what had happened to her.

"Are you kidding?" she wrote back. "Great-grandma married a doctor and held court in the big house over her dynasty of children and grandchildren. When Mary Suzanne visited, it was really sort of romantic."

Although I'd never really known Great-aunt Cathy, I'd been there when her ashes were buried, and I liked knowing she'd had a good life.

By the end of June, I was spending a lot of time at the river with Adam. He had a way of making space for a person to settle into.

"I'd like to plant something out here," I told him one Saturday as we pushed back and forth on the glider behind the cabin.

"You mean something pretty like a flower?"

"Too frivolous. Something . . ." I raised my arms to the sun, filtering through the leaves of the huge oak tree.

"Bigger? A tree?"

"Too permanent. I'm not going to be here that long. Something . . ." I shrugged.

"Beans," he said, barely brushing his lips with mine in a way that drove me wild. "You want to plant beans."

I threw my arms around his neck, demanding a real kiss. The depth of the sky and the true depth of kissing. Two things he'd taught me.

"Why would I want to plant beans?" I asked him later.

"'Cause we could build a tepee for them. Like we do back home. A tepee for the beans to vine up."

"I've seen pictures," I said. "Kind of like the pioneers."

"Pioneers—pfffh. My mama does it every year. Dad builds her the tepees, and she plants the pole beans."

I wondered what Stanza—probably stretched out on the deck flirting with her cousin's friend—would think if she could see me sweating in the woods, helping Adam trim branches and lash them together at the top.

We planted the beans south of the cabin, along the edge of the bluff. Adam dug up the earth, set the poles, and made hills, and I buried the beans and watered them.

"The tepee against the sky looks like a marker," I said. "You know. The big X on the map. *You are here.*"

He held me close, his sweat smelling good. "You are here," he said.

That night, I decided to make tea for Grandpa Jim and me. I was missing my mother's ambrosia. Maybe I was even missing her a tiny bit. As I was making the tea, I splashed hot water on my hand and cried out as the arch between my first finger and my thumb turned lobster red.

"Mona?" Grandpa Jim called. "You all right?"

"My hand. I burned my hand." I squeezed my eyes shut, the tears stinging.

"Here, here," he said, coming to hold my hand under cold water.

I gasped.

"It burns, I know. Come in the bathroom. I have some ointment."

I sat on the stool, and I could tell it hurt Grandpa Jim's leg to balance on the edge of the tub, but he held my hand on his knee and gently stroked on the glistening compound. It hurt so bad I could hardly breathe. I *did* want my mother.

"I spy something blue," Grandpa Jim said. "And it's a pair."

"Your eyes," I guessed. Then I laughed a little despite the pain. "No, my eyes, too."

That night, as I lay in bed, my hand bandaged and no longer hurting, I gazed at the stars through the skylight in the spare bedroom. Some seemed to be fading softly around the edges, others seemed to pulse and dance. As I waited for sleep, I watched, wondering how many Snows had looked at these same stars. And it was odd, but I had the feeling the cosmos was gazing back, whispering to me that it was pleased I was there, if just for a while.